THE LAST NIGHT

STEVE MCELHENNY

All rights reserved.

The characters and events portrayed in this book are fictitious. Any similarity to real persons, living, dead, or even the living dead, is coincidental and not intended by the author.

No part of this book may be reproduced, or stored in a retrieval system, or transmitted in any form or by any means, electronic, mechanical, photocopying, recording, or otherwise, without express written permission of the publisher.

Cover design by Sicaso Publishing

First edition printed 2025

Copyright © 2025 Steve McElhenny

ISBN: 9798315541523

For my creatures of the night, Sian, Sophia, and Carys.

PROLOGUE

The year was 1984.

It may not have been the dystopian future envisioned by George Orwell, but instead the year that Kenny Loggins brought us 'Footloose.'

It was also the year the Ghostbusters saved the world by crossing the streams. Michael Jackson's hair famously caught fire thanks to Pepsi, and Marvin Gaye tragically caught a bullet thanks to his father.

Bruce Springsteen patriotically declared he was 'born in the USA,' whilst Madonna shamelessly informed us she was 'like a virgin.'

Tetris had hit the arcades, draining addicted children and adults alike of their coins, and NASA launched the shuttle Discovery.

More importantly, regarding this tale, it was the year that four teenage boys from the small English town of Hulmsford, in Hertfordshire, spent an ill-fated night in Davenport Manor.

To those reading this, I anticipate the name Davenport Manor won't mean anything to you. Yet, to those who resided in Hulmsford and its surrounding villages, this building was synonymous with tragedy, cruelty, murder and superstition – and, for those four teens on the 8th September 1984, it was to be the place they would spend their last night together.

The motive for these four individuals coming to this foreboding and deserted building had been born from a pact that three of them had made with each other several years prior.

It was an oath that, before they went their separate ways in life, they would spend their last night together inside Davenport Manor. After all, they reasoned, if they could face their fears inside of this place, then they would be able to face any of the other fears the much wider world would be sure to end up throwing at them.

This pact hadn't been the first time such words or intentions had been spoken about by those who knew of the manor's nefarious reputation. For parents scolding their disobedient children, spending a night in Davenport Manor was often levied as an empty threat: 'If you don't eat your vegetables or do your homework, I'll make you spend the night there.' For those wanting to show off their bravado, it was used to elevate their standing amongst their peers: 'I'm going to spend the night in Davenports, just you wait and see.'

It would have seemed by the number of claims from someone having a 'friend of a friend' who once spent the night there that most of the town had been inside this macabre manor at some point. Yet, the truth of the matter was that these threats or intentions were never acted upon – nor were these audacious claims ever believed or substantiated.

The last time this building had been documented as being populated was in 1917 – but I am getting slightly ahead of myself. Please permit me to give you a brief timeline of some key events in Davenport Manor's history – some of which will be elaborated upon as this tale progresses.

10 February 1849 – Construction of Davenport Manor begins deep in the woodlands of Hulmsford Forest at the edict and financing of little-known entrepreneur, Lord Archibald Davenport. It is intended to be his new home following his move from York.

17 February 1852 – Construction is completed, and under Davenport's orders, it instead finds a new purpose as a sanatorium for the victims of a tuberculosis outbreak that has struck Hulmsford. Archibald Davenport is subsequently hailed as a righteous man and the town's saviour.

August 1852 – April 1853 – Several missing persons are reported to the Hulmsford magistrate, Clarence Swift. The missing persons are predominantly male, middle-aged and with little to no family.

4 May 1853 – John Milford, an alleged patient from Davenport Sanatorium, arrives at the doorstep of Clarence Swift – he is fatigued, bloodied, and on the brink of madness.

Milford displays no evidence of tuberculosis; however, he does display significant signs of physical abuse and mental trauma. He claims to have escaped the sanatorium, having been taken from his home in the night by Davenport's staff several months prior, despite showing no signs of illness.

Milford claims to have seen and done things inside the sanatorium that even the devil would baulk at.

Upon preparing a written statement of the events he has witnessed, Milford bites off his own tongue in an attempt at suicide. He subsequently chokes to death.

5 May 1853 – Alarmed by Milford's claims and actions, Magistrate Swift orders members of the local constabulary to pay a surprise visit to Davenport Manor to investigate if there are any truths to these accusations, or if they are just the mere ramblings of a madman.

To their horror, Milford's claims prove true. They find evidence of black magic ritualism, systematic torture and killings of the patients within.

19 May 1853 – Archibald Davenport and his stewards are sentenced to public hanging. Amongst the charges levied against them are murder, abduction, physical abuse, indecency, being in league with the devil, and for generally being all-round dicks. Of those few patients who survived their stay at Davenport Manor, they are relocated to Hill

End Asylum, St Albans, due to their lingering madness and trauma caused by their experiences.

18 November 1916 – Davenport Manor is renamed the Institute for Hope and Glory. It is designated as a rehabilitation centre for commissioned British army officers suffering from extreme psychological trauma from their experiences in the Great War.

5 January 1917 – The first wave of patients are assigned to Hope and Glory.

19 January 1917 – A violent riot breaks out in Hope and Glory, resulting in the deaths of many of the staff and patients alike.

Such is the brutality of this riot, and the extremities of the deaths caused, for a while, the manor takes on the moniker as the Institute for Hope and Gory.

Though the report of the full extent of the events becomes classified, leaked eyewitness accounts claim that in a resident's final moments before their suicide, they utter the words, 'Davenport sends his regards.'

9 May 1940 – An errant bomb lands on the Hulmsford Forest during the Luftwaffe blitz campaign. Much of the woodland surrounding the now-abandoned Davenport Manor is destroyed by fire, yet the building and its grounds inexplicably remain unscathed.

18 October 1956 – Hugh Lancaster, a potential buyer for Davenport Manor takes a tour of the building. Upon completing his inspection, his chauffeur testifies that he observed Mr Lancaster taking the spare jerry can of petrol from the boot of his Rolls Royce and dousing himself before setting his body alight.

1 November 1966 – Local reporter, Gerard Hawkly chokes

to death on a Scotch egg whilst researching Davenport Manor for an upcoming book. There is no evidence that this is anything other than an unfortunate coincidence and a misjudgement of throat-to-egg-size ratio, but the incident only serves to add further superstition and hysteria over the manor's reputation.

Despite this building's woeful history, the local council had no time or prevalence for such fallacy and cursed tales. What scared them the most about this building was the bureaucracy and potential lawsuits over any health and safety failings Davenport Manor surely possessed over its decades of neglect.

With its reputation making itself a Venus fly trap for the curious and the reckless, the council had seen it cheaper to fence it off, complete with a top layer of barbed wire, and have its perimeter manned by a security guard than to spend millions of pounds of their precious local funding to renovate, safe-proof and idiot-proof it – and it soon became apparent there were a lot of idiots in Hulmsford.

Had Davenport Manor been in a more suitable, or logistically sound location other than deep in the forest, which had now replenished itself after its fire four decades earlier, then perhaps the council would have thought differently on the matter. Maybe, they'd have even adopted it as their civic offices. Yet, other than its original purpose as a sanatorium, its site wasn't suited for practicality or convenience.

As such, the mentality of 'out of sight, out of mind' was adopted by them – they only wished that the townsfolk and the curious would adopt the same mindset.

CHAPTER ONE

The lone security guard manning the proverbial fort of Davenport Manor on the night shift of Saturday, 8th September, was Joseph Daley, aged twenty-four. The time was coming up to 23:00.

Joseph had only been on shift for an hour, yet he had already seen himself through two-thirds of the contents of his thermal flask. The night was proving to be as bitter as the cheap instant coffee he had been drinking.

If any comfort was to be found in the wooden security hut, which in all actuality was nothing more than a glorified garden shed, it came from the paraffin heater, which teased him with rations of warmth.

Joseph couldn't regard any of the other compliances in this hut as mod-cons, just straight-up cons. Heck, there wasn't even a Portaloo available—despite his persistent protests.

The council dismissed these reasonable requests as just another additional and unnecessary cost. His superior even went so far as to suggest that if it's such a certainty bears shit in the woods, then it would have to be good enough for him too.

It wouldn't have been so bad if they had provided him with quality toilet paper instead of the cheap and nasty stuff. He often wondered if he'd be better off going full feral and using the leaves of the woodland to wipe his arse with instead. Maybe he'd even use some of this crappy toilet paper—pun intended—to write his inevitable resignation on, and he wouldn't be signing it in ink, that would be for sure.

Despite there being a small analogue alarm clock atop the cramped workstation littered with other clutter and dirty magazines, or the 'Junk n' Spunk' desk as he referred to it, Joseph preferred to check his digital watch for the time instead. It even had an LCD racing game built into it for the particularly tedious nights, which pretty much accounted for all of them.

Though the inside of the security hut's main source of light was limited to the push light stuck to the ceiling, outside, he was reliant on a battery torch—for when he partook in his sporadic patrols around the perimeter.

Still, he didn't need any torch to know it had started raining on this night. The constant patter of heavy drizzle against the roof and solitary window was enough to make its presence known.

Usually, when the weather was like this, it would be even less likely than usual for there to be any incidents or events to report. 'Nothing stifles the bravado of men like a mild bout of bad weather,' he'd mock in his mind.

He checked his digital watch once more; it had become a compulsion since he started this shift.

They were late.

Not that this was a bad thing. With any luck, the rain had dampened their spirits, along with everything else. Maybe they'd had more time to think things through and to see sense. The most likely scenario was they'd chickened out—they wouldn't have been the first to talk a big game over Davenport Manor, only to bottle it come match day.

The arrangement Joseph had made may have been more than his job was worth, but he was under no illusions his job was worth shit. It was minimum-wage employment for minimum job enjoyment.

He likened his shifts to the frequent bouts of isolation he used to receive in school for his regular unruliness, only this was a hell of a lot more miserable. As irony would have it, he was even reading more now on shift than when he was at school. Granted, the racier nature of the books and magazines here weren't exactly the sort he'd find on the national curriculum.

It had been three weeks since his eighteen-year-old little brother had approached him in his bedroom with a business proposition.

The Last Night – Steve McElhenny

'Hey, Joey, have you got your shift patterns for Davenports yet?' Grady Daley had asked.

'Yeah,' he had responded with disdain. 'I got them through a few days ago. Looks like I've been shafted royally again. I'm stuck on the graveyard shift for the next month. Sucks, right?'

He'd observed the mischievous glint in Grady's eyes which informed him this news didn't suck for him as much as it did his big brother.

'Want to make yourself some extra cash?' Grady baited. It was a silly question. What person in their right mind didn't want to make themselves some extra money? The more appropriate question would have been, 'How far are you willing to go to make this extra cash?'

Previously, when Grady had asked him this question, it had more often than not been for disorderly reasons, but it was still easy money, nonetheless. To buy him some booze, or to be a fake alibi for when their parents, and on occasion, the police, came asking questions about his whereabouts at a certain point in time.

Yet over the past few months, that source of additional income had dried up. Now Grady had turned eighteen, he could buy his booze legally and had even seemed to clean his delinquent life up somewhat. This new outlook on life was great for his little brother, he guessed, but it sure did blow for his bank balance. As such, this extra cash being offered didn't exactly scream easy money anymore.

'I'm listening,' Joseph replied. His curiosity was as piqued by the why as to the how much.

'I need you to let myself and three others into Davenport during one of the shifts you're on. 8th September to be precise.'

'What? Why?'

'It's not for me. It's for Ben,' the earnest reply came.

'That's way fucking worse?' Joseph attempted to reason.

The Ben to whom Grady was referring was his new friend, Ben Mills. The sudden friendship they had struck had been as unexpected as it had been unlikely—and tragically, through the cruel twists of life, it would be one never fated to last long.

At seventeen years old, at the behest of shitty genetics, Ben was expected to never make it past the age of eighteen. Since his diagnosis of Leukaemia three years earlier, he had been through all the treatments available. They were no longer seen as curative operations but stalling tactics against the inevitable.

'It's his dying wish,' Grady laid on thickly.

'I thought you said his dying wish was for me to drive you both to the cinema in Welwyn to watch that Elm Street film,' Joseph replied sardonically.

This wasn't the first time Grady and Ben had played the dying wish card on him—it had been reshuffled and dealt back out several times already.

Other instances of his 'dying wish' included Ben borrowing Joseph's Iron Maiden record collection, his porn mags, and even the sacrilegious act of wanting his last Rolo.

Not that Joseph minded, of course; he was happy to play along with them both—how could he say no to that poor dying bastard? And just like Grady, he had quickly developed a soft spot for Ben. Besides, there was never any harm that came from these requests; furthermore, despite his circumstances, he had been a positive influence on his brother. This request, however, was different.

Joseph had never been one to fall foul of the blanket of superstition and hysteria which clouded Davenport Manor—it was probably his indifference to its history that had seen him land the security gig. Yet even he had to concede there was something very off about the place.

As part of his job (at shift end), he would be required to enter the manor—to ensure no one had managed to creep in undetected, or to report back to the council any internal structural damage of concern that may have happened overnight.

When entering the building, he would find himself

rushing through his checks, and even skipping many of them, to ensure he'd never spend more than a dozen minutes at a time inside.

He had still to see anything out of the ordinary or hear any noises that couldn't be explained, but there was still something about this place which set his mind, and his nerves, off-kilter.

The rational side of him reasoned this was just some psychological effect he was subconsciously inflicting on himself.

He had heard the twisted tales of this place just like everybody else in this town. Yet unlike everybody else, he had found himself with a front-row view of the scene of the alleged crimes. How could he not walk through this building and wonder if the spot he was standing on was the same spot where one of those murders had been committed, or tortures performed?

'This dying wish is for real,' Grady enthused, this time with sincerity. 'It's part of some stupid pact he made with a couple of his best friends a few years ago. I gotta tell you, Joey, I've never seen his heart set on something so badly. I genuinely think that if you say no, he'd try some other harebrained scheme to sneak in. At least this way we can do things where we can keep an eye on him.'

'What if his health takes a turn? It's not exactly the easiest of places for an ambulance to get to.'

'I've said all this to him already. Yet he's adamant this is what he wants.'

'I don't like it.'

'If I'm honest with you, Joey, I don't think I do either. But this is the only thing I think he has left to fight for right now. It feels so wrong to break his heart so badly when heart is the only thing he's got going for him these days.'

Joseph could tell his brother was serious about this.

'How much?'

'Excuse me,' Grady replied.

'You said there was to be some extra money in it for me.

The Last Night – Steve McElhenny

If I'm to sell my soul to the devil, it had best be at least worth my while. This isn't just my job we're talking about here; it's my good conscience.'

'Come off it, bro, we both know you'd sell our beloved grandmother into the sex trade if it made you a decent earner out of it.'

'How much?' Joseph repeated, this time with conviction.

'Oh shit, I dunno. A hundred quid, I guess. I can prob get the others to cough up their share.'

'You've got that apprenticeship now, little brother. You can do better than that. Two hundred, and you've got yourself a deal. It is his dying wish after all.'

******

Back in his security hut, Joseph could see through the window a quartet of torch beams dancing with each other as if they were fireflies playing tag, accompanied by the loud sound of laughter as they approached. So much for the boys acting inconspicuous—as were their strict instructions.

Joseph emitted a heavy sigh and grabbed his torch from the Junk 'n' Spunk desk. He pulled up the hood of his anorak and exited the dryness and relative warmth of his hut to greet the quartet.

Grady had been leading the group, with Ben close behind. The other two boys in their company, ever so slightly further back, he didn't recognise.

As his beam of torchlight landed on Ben, Joseph couldn't help but compare him to a ghoul from one of the horror films which had been irresponsibly ever-present throughout their upbringing.

Ben's face seemed even more gaunt and pale than Joseph was used to seeing, possibly in part to the contrasting stark-red anorak he was wearing. His eyes looked sunken behind the dark circles around them, making him look far more aged than his young years would have you believe.

It had been only a couple of weeks since Joseph had last

seen him, and the speed of his deterioration was striking. A terrible knot twisted in his stomach as he couldn't help but feel the six-month life expectancy Ben had been given by his doctors during his most recent consultancy had been grossly optimistic and exaggerated.

It appeared one of the boys Joseph didn't know had drawn the short straw and was carrying Ben's rucksack as well as his own, not that it looked to be any hardship to him.

This boy was of a tall and stocky build. Six foot two tall, muscular and with a Desperate Dan jawline.

His impressive stature was further amplified by the contrasting, gangly, pencil-thin, already balding figure beside him.

They looked as if they could pass off as some vaudeville double act of old, such were their stark differences in physical appearance.

'Hey bro,' Grady called out to him.

'Hey yourself,' he acknowledged.

'Hi Joey,' a weaker voice called out. It came from Ben.

'Hey buddy,' Joseph responded with far more warmth than he had his brother. 'How you holding up?'

'Well enough to kick your arse,' he joked. He mimicked a tongue-in-cheek boxer's stance, which elicited a laugh from Joseph. 'These are my friends, Dale and Callum.'

He gestured to the two others. Dale was the stocky one and Callum the gangly one.

Joseph paid them little further consideration. His focus was on his brother and his terminal friend.

'You two come with me,' he commanded.

Joseph led them to his security hut and gestured for Ben to get himself inside out of the rain and to get warm. Such were the limitations of the confined space; it was not a luxury he offered to Grady, nor took up for himself.

'There's some hot coffee left in the flask if you want some, kid,' he offered.

'I'm okay, thanks,' his soft response came.

'Suit yourself, but this next offer is non-negotiable.'

Joseph reached into the hut and opened one of the drawers at his paltry excuse of a workstation. He pulled out a walkie-talkie and handed it to Grady, who was standing next to him outside the open doorway.

'This is linked up to my walkie in here. The battery is fully charged, so there's no excuse for it not to be on at all times, and until I come and fetch you an hour before my shift ends in the morning—before my cover arrives and starts asking questions. Questions like, why the hell are there four teenagers inside Davenport on my shift? That is, of course, if you guys don't decide to hightail it out of there before then.

In either case, I'll be radioing in to check up on you regularly throughout the night anyway. Got it?'

'Got it,' Grady confirmed.

Joseph's voice lowered in an attempt to not be overheard. It was clear to Ben that he was the subject of the clandestine conversation—something he was getting accustomed to since his diagnosis. Who'd have thought one of the side effects of his illness was that he seemingly turned invisible to others? Another side effect was that people deemed it necessary to talk to one another about his welfare as if he had no say or opinion on the matter.

Some people even talked about him in his presence as if he was already dead.

'If anything happens to him, or there are any sudden shifts with his health, radio through straight away, alright, and we'll figure something out.'

Grady nodded again, smiled and turned to Ben.

'He said if anything happens to you, you're fucked, but we'll try and figure something out anyway.'

Ben smiled back at Grady and gave him the A-OK sign.

That was one of the reasons he liked Grady so much; despite his unfavourable reputation, he was one of the few people who didn't talk to him as if he was a walking lament.

Their friendship had begun out of the blue a few months earlier. However, they had been aware of the other's existence for a long time before that.

Even though they had shared the same school year, due to Ben's academic proficiency compared to Grady's intellectual struggles, they had never shared any of the same classes or playground cliques.

Grady first made a more concerted note of Ben when it had been announced a few years earlier by the headmaster in the school assembly that Ben Mills was going to be absent for a while as he was undergoing treatment for leukaemia, and that everyone in the assembly was to say their deepest prayers for him.

Grady had never been one for praying, especially to a god he didn't believe existed. The way he saw it, he didn't know this kid from Adam, so he wasn't going to start sobbing uncontrollably, like many of the other kids in the assembly were doing.

On occasion, he would see him in the playground following his intermittent returns from whatever bout of treatment he was getting this time around. Out of what little decency he still had left to display on the schoolyard, Grady would exclude him from whatever habitual bullying and tormenting he was participating in that day.

The irony had even struck Grady that he had missed almost as much term time as this poor bastard through his various suspensions - yet the headmaster had never asked the school assembly to say a prayer for Grady fucking Daley. Nor did anyone in that school ever cry over him—they cried because of him for sure, but never over him.

Not that he could have cause to complain about his treatment from the school's head. He suspected that his regular suspensions, instead of the much easier and sensible option of permanent expulsion, was due in large part to the fact that Grady was the school football team's star player. This theory was supported by the fact the head always seemed to schedule his suspensions around their more challenging matches on the fixture list.

Grady was hard-pressed to even think of a time he and

Ben had interacted one-on-one throughout their entire time at school. Granted, Grady had left as soon as he was able at sixteen years old, and to little protest from the teachers, students and even his parents.

He had soon found himself stumbling into a Youth Training Scheme bricklaying apprenticeship for a local building company, on account of one of the foremen being in the same local football team he played for.

Now he was in the big bad world and in the company of adults, he was finding his opportunities to bully and torment had reduced drastically—he'd even been a recipient of it on the building sites. None more so than from his gaffer and his weaselly little crew. Still, he knew he would have to grin and bear it if he wanted to complete his apprenticeship.

Sure, he could have fallen back on a token job in his father's newsagent's, but that was hardly something that appealed to either him or his father. As such, he saw what he'd been given as an acceptable hand—and one he was content to stick with, rather than twisting and going for bust.

With him experiencing what it was like to be on the other end of the bullying food chain, he was spending more and more of his time reflecting on his prior actions and the regrets that came with them. He knew he wanted to be a better person, and for the most part he was doing an acceptable job in succeeding.

It had been an adequately warm June summer evening— or in English weather terms, 'at least it wasn't pissing down'—when Grady and Ben finally did strike up a conversation for the first time.

The location had been the town's recreational field, and Grady had been sitting on the children's swing by himself, swaying back and forth like a petulant pendulum. Each time he rocked, it signified another few seconds his alleged date, Raquel Lewis, was late. She was supposed to have met him here at 20:00; the time was now a little past 20:30.

In hindsight, maybe he should have suggested

something more romantically appealing than a children's park for a first date—but other than her acceptable physique and dark auburn hair, he saw very little else romantically appealing about her.

Besides, in his skewed logic, this was way better than any fancy restaurant. This was the great outdoors...sort of. And if she wanted flowers, there were lots of flowery-looking stuff growing amongst the overgrown vegetation of the field's perimeter he could pick for her.

As for food and drinks? He had a two-litre bottle of Woodpecker cider in his Kwik-Save carrier bag and a Yorkie bar in his jacket pocket. Sure, the advertising campaign on the television stated that it was a chocolate for men only, but he was a feminist and would prove it to her by letting her have some of it—if she truly insisted.

Grady sat gently swaying, resigned to the fact she wasn't going to show and pondering why a stellar catch like himself would be stood up so heartlessly. As a result, he found himself in a lousy mood. The rejection he was feeling this night was proving to be more than enough of a trigger to regress to his reprobate thoughts, and he was locked and loaded to unleash his frustrations on whoever the next people unfortunate enough to wander past him happened to be.

As rare Grady fortune would have it, he saw two boys cutting through the recreation field, and though he couldn't make out their features from their current distance, they looked to be of a similar age to him, and that meant they were fair game to unleash his vexations onto.

Like any good predator, he played it cool.

There was no need to make any sudden movements just yet. He would let the prey come closer to him, not knowing the danger they were nonchalantly ambling into.

Grady continued his gentle rocking on the swing, all the while scrutinising the duo.

As they got closer, he recognised one of the boys immediately. How could he not?

It was that terminal kid.

It seemed that Lady Luck had been the second female to stand him up on this night and had been replaced by her skanky little sister Miss Fortune.

Although Grady was perfectly aware of how much of an arsehole he could be for much of the time, even he wouldn't think of stooping so low as to pick a fight with a kid looking to seek a permanent residence outside of Death's door.

All hope was not lost, however. The termy wasn't alone.

He ran through a checklist in his mind over the other kid to see if they met the criteria for a good old beating.

Were they female? No.

Did they look to have any long-term illnesses? No.

Did they look under sixteen years old? No.

Did they look like they were bigger and stronger than him? A big fat no.

It was a very short checklist.

The duo were close enough to be inside Grady's peripheral now.

He was mulling in his mind over how to approach this. Should he pick an argument first so it would be easier to justify the fight—in case his victim squealed to the police? Or, should he just go straight at it?

'Ah, screw it,' he thought.

He had already used up all his patience waiting on his no-show date.

'Hey you,' he shouted from the swing.

The boy he didn't know instinctively turned his head and, upon recognising Grady, performed a seamless 180-degree turn and began sprinting away. Credit where credit was due, this kid was a speedy little bastard.

Grady attempted to flip off the moving swing in a cool-looking dismount before making his pursuit. Unfortunately for him, his execution left a lot to be desired. He spectacularly misjudged his landing, which resulted in him losing his footing and falling flat on his face.

Though the faceplant had been soft, his machismo had

been hit hard—though not as hard as the returning swing that had sucker-punched him in the back as he stood up. This was turning out to be a doozy of an evening.

To Grady's amazement, however, Ben hadn't followed his friend in retreat. He just stood fixed in place, staring at him curiously.

'Tell anyone about this and you won't live to see your next birthday,' Grady threatened.

'I probably won't live to see my next birthday anyway,' the droll response came. There were no signs of being intimidated present in his voice.

To Grady's further astonishment and infuriation, Ben lifted up a Polaroid instant camera that was hanging from around his neck and took a photo of him.

'What the hell are you doing?' he asked, flustered.

Ben took the photograph that had come from the camera and handed it over.

'It usually takes a few minutes to develop.'

'Why waste a photo on me?'

'It's only wasted if you don't keep it,' the reply came. 'It would be cool though if you did. It would be nice for people to have something to remember me by when I'm gone. I'm not narcissistic enough to take photos of myself, and besides, who the hell wants a photo of me looking like some sick Victorian orphan child? I'd much rather people have a photo of how I see them, as opposed to how they see me.'

'You're pretty weird,' Grady's matter-of-fact response came.

'You want to see something really weird?'

Before Grady could answer, Ben removed the short, black wig from atop his head and then adopted a pose resembling that of Nosferatu from the old black and white movie.

'My name is Nosferatu and I'm here to drink your blood,' he mimicked in a heavy European accent.

Grady chuckled, something he rarely did in the presence of others.

'Very good,' he conceded. 'Though I think you'll find Nosferatu is a silent movie. The voice you're putting on is Bela Lugosi from Tod Browning's 1931 Universal adaptation of Dracula.'

Ben threw him a look that was both surprised and impressed, a look Grady was quick to pick up on.

'What can I say,' Grady continued. 'I know my horror movies. I even have a neat little trick to get myself some tapes that's given me a few belts off my father in my time, but it's totally worth it.

Every so often, I swipe my father's order list for the month's new video tape stock for the newsagent's before he sends it off. I add a few horrors on there without him knowing. My brother and I play interference when the new shipment arrives and hide the extra stock before he's any the wiser.

Of course, he always finds out when he checks the monthly accounts, but by that point we've already watched the films and sold the crappier ones on. I've even got an original VHS of Cannibal Holocaust back at mine; I managed to get it before that whole video nasty nonsense came in.'

'No way!' Ben couldn't contain his excitement. 'Swap it with you for my pirate copy of New York Ripper?'

It was now Grady's turn to look impressed.

'How the hell did you get that?'

'Dying young has its perks. Some kids in my shoes want to run out onto a football pitch with their favourite team as one of their last wishes. Me, I just want to watch depraved Italian horror where the killer pretends to be a duck.'

Grady chuckled again.

'I take it back dude, you're not just weird, you're fucking out there. I like it. You know what, I think I will keep this photo. Maybe you best get on out of here if you want to find that chickenshit friend of yours though. The speed he was legging it, he's probably halfway to Scotland right now.'

'Ah screw him. Any shepherd who abandons his sheep

at the first sign of a wolf is no more a friend than the wolf itself.'

Ben observed the perplexed look on Grady's face as he tried to make sense of the metaphor. Though he thought this would have made an interesting photograph of him, he refrained from taking another picture; he didn't want Grady to think he was mocking him as opposed to being intrigued by him. He was only too aware of his reputation, none more so than from the firsthand accounts of his bullying from his best friend, Callum Green. Yet the person in front of him didn't seem so bad, at least, not to him.

'He's not exactly what you'd call a friend,' Ben continued in simpler terms, more so to break the developing silence. 'I guess he's more of an acquaintance from Chess Club we were just coming back from.'

Grady couldn't help but scoff.

'Chess Club! Wow, and I thought my evening was sucking balls. Well, anyway, it was cool chatting to you, and thanks again for the photo.'

Ben could tell when someone was shutting down a conversation when he heard it and was taken aback slightly. Unlike a room full of amputees, he felt this chat still had plenty of legs.

Nonetheless, he wasn't going to force the matter and slowly began to trudge away.

As Grady observed Ben walking away, fixing the wig back in place on his head, he couldn't help but feel sympathy for the kid. Not because of his illness, but because he could tell that this poor bastard had been wrapped in cotton wool for the last few years when he should have been getting into the scrapes and hijinks that are an obligation for any self-respecting teen.

Maybe, he could be a better version of himself on this night after all—even if that better version meant leading Ben astray.

'Hey, Chess Club,' he called out. Ben stopped, then turned to face him. 'What's say we have some real fun tonight?'

A smile began to find its way onto Ben's gaunt face.

******

The time was approaching 21:00, which meant the Hulmsford Catholic Choir were wrapping up their weekly practice in the church hall. The members mightn't have been old enough to be considered antiquities just yet, but they were certainly vintage.

These days, there were only around twenty of them in their troupe, but what they lacked in numbers, they made up for with enthusiasm.

As they began to exit the church in their cliques, nattering amongst themselves in self-congratulation over a night's practice well done, they were suddenly interrupted by the sound of a high-pitched scream from one of their number.

Her gaze was fixed on one of the many gravestones in the churchyard, and more specifically, the gaunt, ghoulish figure of a young man that had slowly risen from behind it. Twisted and pale, it stood in evident pain.

She and many others made the sign of the cross as they witnessed what they believed to be an unholy apparition. Then, they saw the far more human figure of Grady Daley walking amongst the tombstones, minding his own business.

If truth be told, some of the choir even made the sign of the cross at seeing this delinquent deviant with such a reprehensible reputation at such a young age.

Grady appeared to be walking obliviously towards this figure, who had now turned its attention to him with insidious intent.

'Hey, look out!' one of the women shouted. She had taken the bait far too easily.

The two boys were playing a blinder.

Grady innocently looked over to the choir as if to say,

'What's up?' Then he looked over to Ben, who pounced on him. It was all the boys could do not to laugh as they disappeared out of view behind the gravestones, and Grady began some pantomime screams of pain.

Their efforts not to break into laughter would have been even more strained had they realised some of the choir had retreated into the church out of fear, and a few others to fetch the holy water.

'You ready for the coup de grâce?' Ben whispered.

Grady staggered back to his feet, clasping at his throat, mimicking that he'd been bitten. Then Ben came up from behind him. They both took a moment to survey and appreciate the faces of their traumatised audience before commencing their encore. Grady grabbed at Ben's hair in their latest staged melee and slowly began to pull at it, making it look as if it were providing great resistance. Ben let out a scream of pantomime pain and anguish as the wig was pulled away from his scalp.

Screams were coming from some of the choir now. To their credit, even their screams were harmonised, their practising had clearly been paying off.

The diabolical duo couldn't contain themselves anymore, partly because of the better-than-expected response from their unwitting victims, but partly because they hadn't planned any further into their ploy. As they both began giggling, they even performed a bow to the outraged audience for their curtain call. It wasn't so much a standing ovation they were receiving but a standing exasperation. Ben even managed to take a few Polaroids of their expressions.

After their graveyard guffaws, the two boys found themselves back in the recreation field on the swings. Grady offered his newfound partner in crime some of his Woodpecker cider.

'Best not, thank you,' the begrudging rebuttal came. 'Alcohol would play havoc with my immune system. I can't take the chance.'

'Well duh, Termy. Alcohol plays havoc with everyone's immune system. It's called a fucking hangover.'

'My whole life is a hangover,' Ben sighed.

Grady suddenly bolted upright as if he were a meerkat who had just been alerted to one of its many predators.

'What's up?' Ben spoke with genuine concern and intrigue.

'Can you hear that?'

Ben listened intently but to no avail.

'I don't hear anything, sorry.'

'Ah, my bad then. I thought I heard the sound of someone giving a shit over your self-pity, but I must have imagined it.' Grady gave Ben a playful, yet purposely gentle, punch to his arm. It felt strange not delivering a blow in frustration, anger or insecurity.

Ben looked at him and smiled.

'Thank you for tonight. I needed to feel normal again.'

'Dude, I hate to break it to you, but pretending to be a zombie in a graveyard, scaring sweet old ladies isn't normal. It's kind of fucked up thinking back on it.'

'Well, thank you anyway.'

'Don't sweat it, dude. It's been a better night than I expected.'

'Grady,' Ben spoke, clearly leading up to a question.

'That's my name, Termy, don't wear it out.'

'Do you want to come over to my house sometime next week for some dinner and to watch New York Ripper?'

Grady smiled with sincerity. He'd never been invited over to anyone's house for dinner before, let alone to watch an infamous Giallo movie.

'Let me think about it, dude,' he replied.

******

Grady did come over to Ben's house to watch New York Ripper, and likewise, Ben had gone over to his to watch Cannibal Holocaust.

Over the next few months, many more trashy horror movies were shared—as did their friendship quickly grow. Then, a week ago, whilst finishing Stanley Kubrick's adaptation of The Shining over at the Daley house, their conversation took a turn Grady had not been expecting.

'Not impressed?' Grady asked. His viewing partner had looked underwhelmed throughout the entire film—other than that scene where there was a bit of bush from that lady getting out of the bathtub.

'Not really, just seemed a bit redundant when we've got something that trumps Overlook Hotel in our very own town.'

'Davenport Manor, you mean?'

Ben nodded his head in confirmation.

'You don't actually believe in those stories, do you? Joseph's told you himself, there's nothing to them, and he should know, right? What with him working there an' all.'

Ben said nothing in response to this. His ashen cheeks instead turned a rare flush. It was clear to Grady that he was sulking.

A rare uncomfortable silence was starting to develop between the two.

'So, what d'you want to watch next?' Grady asked in an attempt to restore peace between them. 'We've got Mausoleum or Sleepaway Camp. You're going to lose your shit over the ending of that one.'

Ben seemed disinterested in Grady's question; instead, he had one of his own to ask.

'We're getting to be pretty good friends, right, Grade?'

'Yeah, I guess.'

'Can I share something with you? Something personal?'

'Oh my god, you're not a bummer, are you, like that puff of a best friend of yours, IQ?'

'His name's Callum, and no, I'm not gay. What I'm about to say does involve him though, and my other best mate, Dale Reeves.'

Grady scoffed internally at hearing Dale's name. He'd

had a run-in with him a few years ago, not long after Dale had arrived in Hulmsford from up Yorkshire way. The two of them didn't see eye to eye, it would seem, and it had nothing to do with Dale's superior height difference.

It had been Dale who'd put a stop to Grady's bullying of Callum. He had followed Grady from school one day and had delivered a beating to him.

Despite Grady's reputation, handiness with his fists and also being a school year older, he had been bested easily by the new kid.

It wasn't the beating itself that had bothered Grady—he had been on the receiving end far worse from his father in his time, some of them self-inflicted. What frustrated him was that it had been clear that Dale had been holding himself back throughout the fight—he had plenty more left in the tank to give. His beating had been just a warning.

It was a taste of his own medicine, and he found it had tasted bitter.

'Leave Callum Green alone,' Dale had ordered. 'If I hear you're continuing to bust his chops over his sexuality, then I won't hold back next time. I know you're in the duffer class, but even you can understand what I'm saying, you hear?'

Grady understood him perfectly well.

'So, what is it you want to share?' Grady asked, trying to shift his thoughts away from the pasting his body and pride had taken that day.

'Long story short, the three of us made a pact a few years ago. A pact that before we went our separate ways in the world, we would spend the night together in Davenport Manor. Well, it looks like that time has come.

I don't know whether you know or not, but Dale's enlisted in the army for the Royal Engineers.

His basic training starts on 10th September. Callum's off to uni a few weeks later, and as for me, well, we all know what my future holds—or lack of one.

Anyway, I spoke to those two earlier today to see if they

still wanted to honour the pact, and they're in. I want you to be there too. It would mean a lot to me. It would be my "for real" dying wish to have done this with my closest friends, and I now consider you to be one of them.'

'I'm not sure, dude. I mean, thanks for thinking of me and all, but you know the old saying. Three's a crowd, but four is fucking awkward as hell when two of that crowd hate your guts.'

'I don't think that's an actual saying. Besides, I've spoken to Callum and Dale about you coming too, and they're okay with it, just as long as there's none of your old antics. Anyway, they know getting in there will be easier with you on board, what with your brother being security and all.'

'Is that the real reason you're asking me?'

'Not at all. I want you there, I swear it. Besides, with or without you, we'll be finding a way to get inside.'

******

'Grady!' His brother's stern voice brought him back to the here and now, breaking him from his memories. 'Did you hear what I was saying? This shit's important.'

'Yeah, Joey, I was listening.'

'Then what the hell was I saying?'

'You said to radio through if anything happens.'

'No, you scrotum pole, after that. This isn't the time for you to go off on one of your daydreams. I was talking about the generator.'

Joseph let out a hefty sigh of frustration.

'You know I hate repeating myself. There's a generator inside for the electrics. They still appear to be working fine, but make sure you only have a couple of the lights on at a time. We may be in the middle of a forest, and I've never had anyone from the council come out to check in on me during the graveyard shift, but there's a first time for everything. The last thing I need is for someone to show up and ask me why all the lights are on inside the house. Got it?'

'Got it.'

Joseph reached into his pocket and pulled out a key.

'This is a spare of the front door padlock. I used a key cutter out of town so as not to have any potential questions asked. I'm adding it to your bill.'

'Thanks, Joey.'

'The only other thing is, please just be careful, okay little brother? You believe in this supernatural shit about as much as I do, but still, you can never say never. If anything starts going down that's off, get yourselves out of there as soon as you can, okay?'

'Sure thing.'

'Okay then, let's do this.'

Joseph gestured towards Dale and Callum to join the others. He pulled another set of keys from his pocket. Judging by the number of keys on the ring, this was the master set.

The four teens all looked at each other with nerves and excitement as the padlock to the main security gate of the fenced perimeter unclasped. They were about to head into the main grounds of Davenport Manor.

CHAPTER TWO

The front grounds of Davenport Manor sprawled over a hundred metres in length - and was its equal in width. Not that the four boys could see anything, other than where their torch lights permitted.

The focus of their beams was trained exclusively on the broken and uneven pathway underfoot.

The slipping and tripping hazards of the terrain had been made only worse, due to the soaking caused by the persistent rain.

The numerous cracks of the paving had been besieged by the overgrown and tangled foliage which had usurped and taken over. Ben couldn't help but contemplate that this was the same thing happening to the inside of his body - only where the path had succumbed over decades, his body had deteriorated in just a few years.

Autumn gusts of wind caused a slow dance of the skeletal branches of the ancient oak trees lining up on either side of the crumbled pathway. Though the boys couldn't see these trees, they could hear their creaking. It was from these branches, so it was said, that some of the patients of the sanatorium were strung up and left to die at Archibald Davenport's twisted amusement.

Though no one said it aloud, Ben was sure the others were thinking the same as himself. Were the creaking noises the wind in the trees? Or was it the spirits of those who were damned to die here? Their bodies cursed to swing forever from the branches which housed the nooses around their helpless necks.

Callum and Dale were about a dozen metres behind the other two.

Although Dale couldn't see his best friend's face through the darkness, he could still picture the disdain upon it as the intense gaze burnt a metaphorical hole into the back of Grady fucking Daley.

Dale put his arm around him in a gesture of solidarity and reassurance, yet the sharp intake of startled breath Callum produced only served to inform Dale he had just made him jump with fright.

'Oops, sorry,' whispered Dale. 'You okay?'

'I'll be fine,' he assured.

Dale had always been protective of Callum - and had been even before he'd formally met him.

******

Callum had already been involuntarily outed as gay at the age of fourteen, and by the time Dale had arrived in Hulmsford from up North with his mother and a promise of a fresh start.

Upon Dale's introduction to the playground by the classmate nominated to show him around his new school, he had been given the pecking order on all the misfits as if they were nothing more than a pack of Top-Trumps.

There was the kid who ate his snot, the kid who stank of piss, the kid who everyone thought was too weird to talk to, and the prize of the bunch, the kid who had been discovered to have been gay.

This being the 1980s, where attitudes, understanding and acceptance were lacking, coupled with a schoolyard where juvenility and peer pressure were rife, it made Callum an instant pariah.

He had also become an irregularity when it came to his school nickname of IQ, in that though it had remained the same for years, it had taken on two different identities in its relatively young lifetime – much like Callum himself.

It had been used as a compliment before his being outed and used to deride him after it.

He had been monikered IQ at the age of twelve as a result of his astonishingly impressive intellect. There was even talk he had been given a Mensa test to take by one of his curious teachers and had scored high enough to be one of its members.

Yet, once word had spread like wildfire that he was a fruit, the school bully, Grady Daley, had changed the abbreviation of IQ from Intelligence Quotient to Incredible Queer.

Alas, for Callum, the proverb of 'sticks and stones' proved to be a bigger falsehood than Gobots being better than Transformers. As many of his fellow pupils' tormenting inevitably graduated from name-calling to physical onslaughts, Callum found himself best placed to conclude that both carried an equal amount of hurt.

For someone as academic as he, much of his life he had spent studying. It didn't matter what the subject or the source was; he was insatiable in his appetite to devour more information and knowledge.

The text to the books he would regularly find himself digesting with ease was black and white and matter-of-fact. There was logic and reason behind their words and diagrams, they gave him comfort. Yet the stark shift of behaviour towards him from those he'd once called friends was confusing him.

He was still the same person they'd once laughed with, played with and studied with, so why all this sudden animosity and ridicule?

As time went on and the novelty wore off, the taunts - to his face at least - simmered down for the most part. Originality and patience were not suitable traits for the ignorant. There were exceptions to this rule, however, and his name was Grady fucking Daley. Though he was an ignoramus of the highest order and not the brightest lightbulb in the hardware store, he was certainly tenacious in his tormenting.

It had been Grady's handiwork which was the cause for the black eye Callum was sporting when Dale had first observed him on the playground, reading a bulky textbook and sitting by himself.

Upon enquiring with his teen tour guide who it was that

had caused the shiner, he had been given Grady's name.

The same day, after school, Dale followed this bully home and gave his physical warning to him to leave the boy alone.

Word of this shining knight, whom he hadn't even met before but had defended his honour, made its way back to Callum the following day in the schoolyard, courtesy of some inadvertent eavesdropping. As such, out of as much intrigue as it was gratitude, he felt obliged to talk to this new kid.

As visible as Dale was on the playground during the morning break time, Callum still had a difficult time approaching him. Not because of any nerves over talking to this mysterious stranger but because of the company that had latched onto him. It had been a handful of the school's rugby team, most significantly, the team's captain, Bradley Hale. Why couldn't it have been anyone but him?

It was because of Bradley his homosexuality had been revealed. Not that he could lay the blame at Bradley's feet for his outing. For someone so intelligent as he was, he could only curse himself for doing something so stupid and reckless.

Callum had left his rucksack unattended whilst kicking a football around with some of his mates on the playground that fateful morning.

One of his classmates, who'd elected not to join in the kickaround, had spotted the aforementioned rucksack and saw too much of a perfect opportunity to squander.

This classmate, you see, had failed to complete his homework in time for the morning's history class - he instead preferred to use his time trying to beat Manic Miner on the C64.

He'd held very little doubt the model pupil, IQ, would not only have completed his homework, but he'd have done it to the highest standard. The classmate was also sure, had he asked IQ, he would have only been too pleased to have given him a quick summary of the homework. Yet, he was too busy kicking the football around, and time in this situation was a precious commodity. Besides, a quick summary for this assignment wouldn't cut the mustard.

He opened up Callum's rucksack undetected with the intention of retrieving the history exercise book. As he rummaged through the bag's contents, he found a notebook that was not school issue and not labelled with any subject.

The curiosity was too much for him to resist - and besides, if he'd already stooped so low as to sneak through his bag to plagiarise his homework, he might as well go the full hog and nose through his other work too.

As he flicked through the pages, he was left with a twinge of disappointment when he saw the book was filled with drafts of poetry and short stories. This was nothing revelatory to the classmate since Callum excelled like he seemed to do with every other subject, at Creative Writing.

He was about to place the book back where he had found it when something caught his eye on one of the pages. A name. It was Bradley Hale's. The page appeared to contain not just a poem, but an ode, and there was a sentence within which sealed IQ's fate on the playground that day.

> May my broken heart forever wail
> Over how you will never love me like I do you
> My soul bleeds for you, Bradley Hale.

The classmate was stunned by what he had read and had instantly forsaken the initial reason he had been inside Callum's backpack. This revelation was worth a thousand detentions, and for the next few minutes at least, he would be coronated as king of the playground for what he had in his possession.

As he excitedly showed the exercise book to a couple of kids nearest to him, word began to spread like a snowball rolling down a hill - and by the time Callum had realised what was going on, that snowball had become the size of the boulder chasing Indiana Jones in Raiders. Only Callum didn't want to run away from it, he wanted it to fatally crush him as badly as the laughs and finger-pointing were crushing his spirits.

To this day, the pupils of Hulmsford Comprehensive School had only ever seen Callum cry twice in the schoolyard. The first was when he had received the news his lifelong best friend Ben Mills wasn't going to be successful in his treatment, and the second time was when his secret had been oh so cruelly revealed.

Despite everyone else's efforts and name-calling since, none more so than Grady Daley's, he swore they would not make him cry again. His heart did indeed wail that day, though not over Bradley Hale - who was amongst those who were prominent in his insults - but because of the cruelty and frailty of those he once thought were friends. The only one who'd unequivocally had his back through all of this was Ben, but with all the adversities he was facing, his time in school was increasingly scarce.

It was when his thoughts turned to his best friend, which were increasing in frequency these days, they put his own life into perspective.

In a few years, he'd be going to a university of his choice on a likely scholarship and away from this town and these people forever. A place where people's opinions weren't as neanderthal and bigoted. Ben would never have that opportunity, yet he still fought hard every day, and for what? A few extra months in this shit hole?

Callum felt ashamed. His best friend was staring death in the face every time he looked in a mirror, yet he couldn't even go and walk over to someone to say thank you, just because they were standing next to an arsehole you once liked. Well, not today.

With a newfound purpose, he made his way with confidence over to Dale - and if there were to be snide comments thrown his way from the others, so what? It wouldn't been anything he hadn't heard already. Besides, he had a feeling this new kid was different.

As he strutted over, he saw Dale was already coming over to meet him halfway.

'Wait, you're not a bummer too, are you?' Callum could hear Bradley challenge the new kid.

'No, I'm straight,' Dale dismissed in a level tone, not even looking behind him. 'I'm just not a judgemental prick like most others in this school, it would seem.'

Callum couldn't help but let out a little chortle to himself as he overheard this, despite his edict to play it cool.

Dale could also hear the group's scoffing but paid them little regard.

'Hey,' said Callum as they formally met. He extended his hand to shake.

'Ey up, fella,' replied Dale in his Yorkshire accent.

'I heard about what you did to that prick Grady fucking Daley, and I wanted to say thank you.'

'Don't sweat it mucka. It's one thing I can't abide is bullies. Never have, never will.'

'Yeah, I've kinda grown to have a distaste for them too, funnily enough.'

Dale let slip a trace of a smile.

'So, what is there to do around this town? It seems pretty dead around here. That lad, Will, who was showing me around yesterday, mentioned something about a haunted house in the woods or something? Sounds pretty interesting.'

'It's called Davenport Manor, and the reason why it's the most interesting thing about this town is because a lot of it isn't true.'

'Yeah, I get that. We had a haunted house back in my hometown of Barndable too. It was an old, detached house on one of the hills on our outskirts. You wanna hear the story?'

Callum nodded.

'A few of us had seen her at some point—the old lady in the

window, that is.

To begin with, it had never crossed any of our minds she was a ghost. I mean, why would it? As far as we were concerned, she was simply just a nosey old housebound lady peering out from behind her bedroom curtains, staring out at the goings-on in the town below.

Most of us who had cause to make the short trek up that hill and to her door for things such as paper rounds and grocery deliveries had come to get used to seeing her and just chose to ignore the stares. Most of us went out of our ways to not even look up at her window anymore, out of fear of being seen to be as equally nosey as she appeared to be.

Then, one day, one of the kids on the playground, a lad by the name of Jason Biggs, told us his remarkable tale.

I use the word 'remarkable' instead of 'unbelievable' in this instance on account of Biggsy being an honest sort. He was not the type of kid to embellish or tell porkies. We used to joke that he had such a strong moral compass and affinity for telling the truth, he'd have made an awful Catholic, as he'd have spent most of his free time in the confession booth.

Those of us who knew Biggsy the best knew that, aside from his family, he loved two things most in his young life: his Raleigh Tomahawk bike and his pet dog, a Labrador by the name of Guess. It was an odd name for a dog, but it gave him some cheap laughs when people asked what it was called.

'Guess,' he would answer.

'Oh shucks, I don't know, Rex, maybe?'

'No. Guess.'

'Fido?'

'Nope. Guess.'

And so the conversation would go round in circles, sometimes for minutes at a time, until the proverbial penny would finally drop.

So when Guess had gone missing for a couple of days,

The Last Night – Steve McElhenny

Biggsy was understandably distraught.

On the advice of his parents, after having no luck in trying to find him throughout the town, he had a flyer made up to stick to the notice board of the local supermarket. They had got the idea from seeing a similar flier for a missing pet cat a month or so previously.

A week passed with no response. Unperturbed, Biggsy printed a whole stack of these flyers to place around town. It was a picture of Guess with the words underneath: 'Have you seen this dog? Reward for his return.' They looked like those wanted posters from old westerns. Some rapscallions even went so far as to graffiti bandit moustaches onto the dog's picture.

Another week passed, and still no leads over the whereabouts of the dog came. Everyone suspected the worst, Biggsy's parents included. Yet he remained resolute.

Instead of putting more flyers up, he got hundreds more made and posted them through every house in town.

Another week passed and with the same result, or lack thereof. His tenacity was finally beginning to waver.

Then the realisation dawned upon him—there was still one house in the town he had not posted a flier to: the house on the hill. He was aware it was a long shot for sure, but when enough long shots are fired in life, the law of averages dictates one of them will have to hit the target eventually.

He mounted his beloved Tomahawk, grabbed one of the surplus flyers and began to pedal to the house on the hill.

Upon reaching the garden gate of the isolated house, he took a look up towards the upstairs window. He had heard on the playground from those of us who had paper rounds about the old lady who was always in the window and how she liked to stare. Just as he'd been told she would be, she was there and staring at him.

Biggsy, being the polite lad he was, knew it was rude to stare back, yet as their eyes locked, he couldn't help but do so. If anything, he was desperate to break their gaze as there was something inherently malevolent about the way she was staring at him. This wasn't a simple stare of curiosity, annoyance, or even resentment over his youth. This was a stare of hunger.

Biggsy found himself wanting nothing more than to turn and mount his trusted steed, the Raleigh Tomahawk, and get away from this house, but his legs felt as though they had turned leaden. He was unable to move, much the same way a rabbit is frozen in place by a pair of oncoming headlights. There was more chance, he felt, of moving Mount Olympus than his skinny twelve-year-old legs.

With him being unable to flee, nor avert his gaze, Biggsy began to notice something about the old lady in the window. Something he had never noticed before, something he wondered if anyone had ever noticed before. She never blinked. Not even once. How was this possible? He began to consider her further.

It wasn't just her eyes that never blinked or moved; it was her expression too. Her complexion was drained of any colour, as if she was a corpse—as if she was a ghost.

He tried to dismiss these thoughts as nothing more than the over-imagination and folly of youth, yet he couldn't shake the feeling there was something so profoundly wrong about the old lady in the window.

Then he found his legs had moved after all, only he hadn't been aware of it. He realised he was several steps closer to the house.

He had opened the garden gate and was on the path without even being aware of his actions. He was being lured up the path like a magnet.

Panic was starting to overcome him now, yet he was unable to avert his gaze from her, unable to run away. The old lady in the window still didn't blink, nor did her expression twitch.

He was closer to her front door now.

Due to the changing angle his closer proximity brought with it, their locked gaze had been broken. Not that it mattered anymore—it was a voice in his head directing him now, a repetitious slither which was neither male nor female. Nor did it sound human at all.

'Welcome home, child. Welcome home, child. Welcome home, child.'

Biggsy couldn't fight these words. Even though he knew it would mean the death of him, he felt compelled to oblige. Just like the voice suggested, he was sure he would be welcomed into the home. He was even more certain he would never leave it.

Had it not been for the sudden sound of a dog barking from within the house breaking him from his trance, then he held no doubt he would have gone inside. Yet this piercing bark was enough to break the spell. He recognised the bark in an instant. It belonged to Guess; he was sure of it.

Yet as much as he loved his missing dog, the fear and the primal instinct for survival took over as he fled.

That night, Biggsy had been unable to shake what he had seen and heard. Had he really seen a ghost? Had he really heard Guess?

The sense of guilt overpowered his fear. If it was his dog inside that house, he had to save it.

Despite it being night, he donned a pair of sunglasses in the hope it would act as a shield from the old lady's hypnotic and insidious stare. To help drown out that serpentine voice, he put on his headphones and inserted a fresh set of Duracell batteries and a Kool and the Gang cassette into his Walkman. He waited for his parents to fall asleep, then snuck out of his home and rode his Tomahawk back to the house on the hill.

When he reached the garden gate of the house, he turned off the bicycle light that had guided him. The only source of light available now was the faint trace coming from behind the upstairs window. Though the curtains were now closed, he could still see the head of the old lady peering out from a gap between them.

Biggsy chided himself in his mind—what on earth was he doing? This was lunacy.

He readied himself to return home and sneak back into bed undetected by his oblivious parents, but then he saw something curious enough to prolong his retreat.

A stray cat brushed past him, causing Biggsy to jump. It appeared to be heading into the garden.

Despite his better judgement, Biggsy turned the bicycle light back on and directed it at the garden to observe the feline. He was struck by the cat's fur standing up on its back as it continued its walk up the path. Just as he had been earlier, the cat's gaze was fixed on the old lady in the window.

As the cat approached closer, the front door to the house began to slowly creak open of its own accord. Biggsy dared to remove his sunglasses for a more focussed and unhindered view. True enough, there was no one in the doorway. Furthermore, the old lady's head peering out from the curtain was still fixed in place.

His attention returned to the stray; it was moving towards the house seemingly against its will. Whatever the house had in store for the tabby, it had intended for him earlier that day. He was aware of the term, 'curiosity killed the cat,' yet in this case, a more apt adage would be stupidity killed the boy.

Biggsy clenched at the handle of the kitchen knife he had brought for his protection, not that he was sure a blade would be effective against what he believed to be a spectre.

In any case, he took a deep breath to help steady his nerves and began to follow. The fact he was doing this of his own free will was troubling enough, but he had to know the truth about this old lady in the window. He had to rescue Guess.

He tiptoed up the short garden path as if he were some kind of pantomime villain from an old silent movie, and despite the fear and nerves overcoming him, he still had the sense of mind to pick up a relatively large stone from the path that was the size of both his fists clenched together.

His intended use for this stone was as a makeshift doorstop. He had seen the front door open of its own accord; what if it were to close shut again by itself too? If so, he needed something to stop it shutting completely and trapping him inside.

He placed the large stone down on the threshold by the foot of the frame and tentatively made his way through the hallway. The cat made its way up the staircase now; it was still visibly resisting its own movement. It knew full well it was heading towards its death.

'Don't worry,' Biggsy spoke to the cat in his mind as he cautiously followed a few steps behind. 'You've got the luxury of nine lives. This poor sucker only has one.'

Biggsy pondered for a moment whether he would be better served by playing saviour to this stray, by picking it up and fleeing the house right now. Maybe he would claim the cat as his own. It may not have been his beloved Guess, but it would make an acceptable consolation prize. Yet, the boy's stomach twisted itself in knots. Who was he fooling? He could never love this cat as much as he loved Guess.

Biggsy braved moving one of the foam-covered earpieces of his headphones from over his ear. Although he didn't want to risk the serpentine voice invading his mind again, he still needed to have his wits about him too. Besides, the upbeat chipper sounds of Kool and the Gang seemed to be mocking him with sarcasm right now.

'Celebrate good times, come on,' the chorus rang. Fuck you Kool and your stupid gang. These are not good times, this is not the time, nor the place for any celebration.

His movement up the stairs was slow and deliberate. He kept to the side of the staircase so as not to risk any careless creaking.

His heart jumped through shock as the silent tension was shattered by a horrific mewl of pain. It was the stray.

Every instinct inside of Biggsy was telling him to run and to do it now, yet he wouldn't leave without Guess. He stayed steadfast in scaling the staircase; he had come this far after all.

He peeked his head around the landing and saw it was clear, yet the bedroom door at the end of it was wide open.

Biggsy could see by the bedroom window the back of the old lady's head, peering out from her usual spot. Yet there was something so very wrong about her. Though the corner of the room was steeped in darkness and shadows, he was almost certain there was no body attached to her head.

'Welcome home, child,' the serpentine voice slithered.

From out of the darkness, the creature fully revealed itself.

Attached to the severed head of the old lady was a tentacle-like limb.

The creature's bare torso was formed from the rotting remains of several animals of varying sizes and species. Cats, rodents...dogs.

Biggsy couldn't help but let out a cry as he saw the matted face of Guess forming the torso's tapestry of remains. He was still alive, but barely. It let out a weakened bark as it noticed his best friend.

The creature's other tentacle had grip of the stray cat and was pushing it into a darkened space on its unholy body. The cat's mewing was more frantic and pained now as it became a part of the creature.

'It's so nice to have a guest over for dinner,' the voice slithered as this abomination moved forward towards the boy.

The head atop this atrocity looked to be ill-fitting, much like a poorly placed toupee.

Its face was one that Biggs could vaguely recall seeing before. It was the door-to-door salesman who had tried pitching an insurance scheme to his parents several months prior. His parents had turned him away in double-quick fashion upon his visit - it would seem some households were far more welcoming.

Though it sickened Biggsy to look at the creature, he was mesmerised by it. He could see on the stomach area, amongst all the other remains of the animals it had been feeding on, a mouth-like shape opening up, its teeth were razored fangs, jagged and yellow. This was where the creature was feeding from.

'Come to me child, be a part of me forever,' the voice slithered.

Not wanting to take any chances with the creature's voice penetrating his psyche again, the paperboy placed the headphones back over both ears again, cranking the volume up for extra measure.

The creature swung its tentacle arm with the old lady's head fixed to the end of it so it locked eyes with the boy. He quickly made a fumble into his pocket for his shades, yet the nerves of the situation were enough to see him drop them.

'That's good, embrace your fear child, fresh meat always tastes better when it is scared.'

The head of the old lady inched closer to him now; he could already feel his sense of resistance drifting away with the trance. Pretty soon he would be a part of this abomination.

Biggsy could feel his legs frozen to the spot. He was no more than a sitting duck - a lobster in a tank at a fancy restaurant waiting to be picked up and picked apart.

Yet there was one last roll of the dice for him.

Though his legs were redundant, he still had use of his hands. He reached into the inner pocket of his coat and withdrew the kitchen knife, thrusting it into one of the eyes of the old lady's head.

A primal roar of pain came from her decapitated head. Encouraged by this reaction, Biggsy withdrew the blade and lunged forward, driving it into the area of the creature which had been used to feed. The creature let out another bellow. It was weakened.

Tears began to stream down Biggsy's face now, as he knew he had one more thrust of the blade to perform.

'I'm sorry,' he addressed what remained of Guess. 'I love you, boy.'

He thrust the blade into the part of the torso which had become infused with his pet.

The whimper of the dog was overwhelmed by the deep roar of pain of the creature as it began to retreat into the shadows. Biggsy could feel his legs again and was only too eager to use them to retreat from the house.

When he told his parents what had happened the next morning over breakfast, they didn't believe him at all, and how could they?

Even when he showed them the kitchen knife covered in a black substance which smelt like rotted meat, they laughed it off as some kind of prank.

Many of the kids on the playground thought it was merely a crazy story too and didn't put much stock into it.

Like all tales though, things evolved, got changed and elaborated upon as they spread.

These stories eventually made their way to the ears of a local policeman, and though he didn't believe a word of it about the creature and the missing pets and salesman, he still thought it best to check on the welfare of the old lady in the window as part of a courtesy call.

There had been no answer when he knocked, though the rotting smells coming from within the house raised enough concerns for him to break down the door.

He found her corpse in her bedroom by the window. There were no signs of any ungodly creatures, no signs of any foul play, or decapitated heads. Her death was deemed to be from natural causes and no foul play suspected.

But here's the funny thing. From the state of the decomposition of her body, the coroner deduced she had been dead for about three months. Those of us who had delivered papers and groceries to her door had seen her face in the bedroom window, staring out at us, many times after it was stated she had died.'

'Holy shit,' Callum proclaimed at the end of the new kid's story. 'No offence, but that's got to be one of the most far-fetched things I've ever heard.'

'No offence taken, fella. Had I not seen the old lady in the window for myself long after she had been estimated to have died, I'd be inclined to agree with you.'

'Still, there's got to be a rational explanation.'

'Aye, most likely. There often is. But why ruin a perfectly good story with simple logic? Sometimes it's far more fun in life to just believe.'

'Well, either way, I enjoyed your tale. I have a best friend, Ben, who would love to hear it too. He loves all that macabre stuff. If you want to hear the best telling of the history of Davenport Manor, he's your man. He's become kinda obsessed with it ever since his illness. I'm sure there are better things to focus on as a distraction, but any distraction is better than the inevitable, I guess.'

'Oh yeah, Will mentioned him too. Poor lad. That sucks balls big time.'

'I'm off to visit him after school if you'd like to come with me. I think you two would get on incredibly well actually.'

'Er, sure, it's not like I've got owt else to do.'

Just as Callum had suspected, Dale and Ben hit it off immediately. It was the friendship version of love at first sight. Their shared dry sense of humour and Dale's matter-of-fact manner made it easy for Ben to open himself up to, something he didn't do with many people anymore - and before long, the new kid became a frequent fixture in the Mills' household. Often visiting with Callum, and often without.

So close had the three of them become, their pact had been made one night when Ben had been discussing a new non-fiction book of ghost stories he had ordered from the local bookshop and saw a page on Davenport Manor within.

Seeing the reference to Davenport Manor, no matter how brief, was like seeing someone you know make a background appearance on a well-known TV show, or in the crowd of a televised sports event – it shouldn't really mean anything, yet the sudden surge of excitement can't be denied.

'We should do it, guys,' he spoke after his verbal dissection of the book's passage. 'We should spend the night there before we go our different ways in life, I mean.'

'Yeah, sure thing buddy,' Callum complied almost robotically and with undeniable sarcasm.

This wasn't the first time the two of them had partaken in similar conversations - the only difference now being that Dale was an audience to it.

'I mean it this time, as in really mean it. Do you know what I'm scared of most if my remaining treatments don't work for this goddamn illness?

It's not so much the act of dying. It's the thought of knowing there'll be so many things I'll be robbed of getting the chance to do. That's the bit that's really not fair, the shit load of regret I'm forced to deal with through no fault of my own. Missed opportunities are something I should have to reflect on when I'm an old man, not when my life has barely begun.

Look, it is what it is. Many of these things I'm never going to be able to do are out of my hands. Me spending a night in Davenport, however! Now that I can control.

Do you know what the scariest thing to me really is about that place? It's not the building, or all the stories which go with it. The scariest thing about that place for me is that I'll end up being just like all the other people in this town who are all talk but never have the conviction to nut up or shut up. If I do nothing else with what could be the short life I have left, I can at least do that. I can be known as the kid who stayed the night in Davenport Manor instead of just being known as that poor bastard who got Leukaemia. I'd also want to spend it with you guys before you get to leave Hulmsford.

Think about it. If you can spend a night inside there, the

scariest thing we know, then you'd be able to face whatever else life throws at you, right?'

'Yeah, OK, I'm game,' said Callum. He had been suitably motivated by his best friend's speech. 'I can't think of a more poetic way to stick it to the arseholes of this town. The faggoty fruit who was more than man enough to do what no one else in Hulmsford had the balls to do.'

'If you two fellas are in, I'm game too,' said Dale. 'Do we need to make a blood oath, or something?'

'Fuck no,' Ben spoke dryly. 'I need all the red blood cells I've got as it is.'

And so the pact was made, and the promise renewed with regularity that their last night together, whenever it would be, they would spend it in Davenport Manor.

******

For the year of 1984, the trio of friends anticipated their last night together would have been the last weekend of September before Callum set off for Cambridge University, to commence his degree in Bio-Chemistry.

Yet, in June, whilst playing Horace Goes Skiing on the Spectrum 48k in Ben's bedroom, Dale casually dropped his bombshell.

He had enlisted in the Royal Engineers, and his basic training was scheduled to begin on 10th September that year.

The date they had planned to break into Davenport Manor may have changed, but the oath had not.

Then, the next bombshell came.

One neither Callum nor Dale saw coming. Ben had made a new friend. Grady fucking Daley.

'Have you gone soft in the head, mucka? Have you forgotten all he's done to our best mate?' Dale snapped upon raising the subject with Ben. It was seldom he raised his voice or lost his temper, so when he did, you knew he was more pissed than a catheter. 'He made Callum's life hell for over a year.'

'No, I haven't forgotten,' Ben said. 'But he's really trying to be a better person, I can see it.'

Neither Dale nor Callum were convinced.

What followed over the course of the next few months felt like some kind of weird custody agreement over Ben. For Callum, he likened it to when his parents separated soon after his being outed. Unlike with his parents, however, although there was bitterness present, it wasn't exactly a battle. He had even overheard his father shout cruelly to his mother once, 'As far as that boy's concerned, it's the loser of the custody battle who gets to keep him.'

With Ben, an unspoken schedule had been devised between them. Callum and Dale would get to hang with him Mondays, Wednesdays and Fridays, and Grady fucking Daley would get him Tuesdays and Thursdays.

Were Callum and Dale happy about it? No, they weren't. Not one fucking bit, but Ben seemed to be, and that's all that mattered to them. Before long, his friendship with Grady fucking Daley was something the other two accepted. Like a bothersome mole, Grady was stuck to him now, and to get rid of him without any unnecessary pain was more trouble than it was worth.

Then the conversation came that Callum and Dale were dreading.

'Is it okay with you guys if Grady comes with us to Davenport Manor? It would mean a lot to me for him to be there with us. Besides, it will be a hell of a lot easier for us to make it inside if he's with us - what with his brother working there and whatnot. We can quite literally waltz right on in.'

Dale let out a huge sigh to show his frustration and displeasure before speaking.

'You know my opinion on the matter, fella. But it's not really my decision, nor should it be yours. It should be that of the lad he's wronged the most.

Callum, what do you think, mucka? Do you want him to

come?'

Callum said nothing for a few moments. His internal deliberations and consequences no matter which decision he made were clear upon his face.

'He can come,' Callum eventually and begrudgingly declared.

'Thank you,' Ben spoke, relieved.

'Just so we're straight, I'm not saying he can come through any forgiveness or compassion. The guy can rot in hell for all I care. Yet I do agree with you when you say we need him if we're to get inside Davenport without any trouble. And if he starts any of his nonsense, believe me, my decision can change with far more ease.'

******

The beams of Dale's and Callum's flashlights stopped at the heels of the other two. They had come to a halt, indicating their destination had been reached. The four boys began moving their torch beams across the fascia of the building in front of them. They had seen pictures of the manor before, in various books on haunted Britain, and at the library in local history books and archives, so they knew what it looked like. Yet this was different. This was real.

The scattershot and undisciplined torchlight allowed teases of the manor's features - much like a seasoned exotic dancer in the early stages of a striptease - only allowing the slightest sight of flesh to playfully taunt their observer into more excitement. Yet also like an aged stripper, it was clear the house's best days of beauty were behind them.

The once vibrant, stained-glass windows which once displayed themselves with all the pride and colour of a peacock had succumbed to a thick layer of grime and looked clouded and dazed under the scrutiny of the torchlight. They were like vacant eyes staring out at the boys. The wooden panel of the front door was lacquered with a flaking and faded red paint which was performing its last stand of defiance against the twin assaults of the elements and the woodworms. The padlock hanging from a bolt was surely more for aesthetics than any practicality since any show of force against the door would result in it feebly submitting in embarrassment.

A collective sense of dread and wonderment came over the quartet. This wasn't fanciful talk anymore. They were actually here. Dale took the lead, placing his foot on the first of the four wooden steps which led up to the doorway. The sound of creaking underfoot as he put his weight upon it, along with the feel of it bowing, instilled little confidence that the inside of the building would be in any better condition. It wasn't so much the prospect of any supernatural entities that would be the death of him, he pondered, but the physical state of the manor.

Ben was far more eager to join Dale at the top of the steps. Even without the weight of his rucksack, Dale couldn't help but notice the step didn't creak or bow as much when Ben stepped onto it. He may have been above average height, coming in at about five-foot-ten, yet Dale estimated his cherished friend couldn't have weighed much over eight stone these days.

With the two of them standing on the top step now, and with Dale in possession of both his and Ben's backpacks, they could feel the step taunting them with the creaking of its strain. Dale didn't want to brave them both crashing through the steps, and risk Ben cutting himself on the wooden shards. The risk of infection with his drastically weakened immunity system was too much. He quickly grabbed the key from Ben, unlocked the padlock, and then pushed the door open.

The sound of the door abrading painfully as it opened almost sounded like it was challenging the boys to enter - if they dared. Ben couldn't help but compare this exaggerated noise to those on the badly dubbed VHS horror movies he had seen far too many of.

They had both taken just a couple of steps inside when

their collective hearts jumped a beat. A sound of something snapping pounced at them from behind. The noise was followed by the more familiar, and strangely reassuring, sound of Grady letting loose with a tsunami of curse words.

They turned around to see him submerged up to his waist. The wooden steps had seen fit to see through their threat to give way. Knowing this foul-mouthed tirade was one born out of anger rather than any pain, the others allowed themselves a not-so-little laugh at their companion's expense. Dale trained his torch light on him, purposely aiming it into his eyes as a subtle cheap shot, and Ben even took the Polaroid camera hanging from his neck and took a snap, the light of the flash adding more duress to him.

Grady became more agitated as he could feel the hands grabbing him from behind. It was Callum trying to pull him up.

'What the fuck? Don't go grabbing anything that will give you cheap kicks,' he snapped.

Callum wasn't in the mood to bite from Grady's tormenting.

'Have it your way,' he spoke purposely nonplussed. His display of indifference to the bigoted outrage only served to heap further ire onto Grady. 'I can just leave you here to struggle whilst the rest of us are inside in the dry. Personally speaking, I prefer that option. Or, you can swallow your pride and accept the help from this incredible queer. Either way, it's no skin off my nose.'

Grady tried pushing himself up from the hole, but with the extra weight of his backpack - at least that was his excuse - he knew it was an attempt fated for failure.

'Fine,' he rued with bitterness.

With the joint efforts of Callum and himself, they were able to pull him up and free, though, in the process, Grady's pride and machismo had been just as destroyed as the step.

CHAPTER THREE

The four of them were now inside the building. The air inside was thick with the overwhelming scent of dust, mildew, and ammonium - an odour accentuated by the darkness that still surrounded them, save for the restricted sanctuary of their torchlight.

'Eww. What's that stench?' Grady asked.

'Ammonium,' Callum responded immediately, pre-empting the inevitable question. Although he couldn't see it in the darkness, he anticipated the look of confusion on Grady's face. 'Piss,' he clarified in far simpler tones. 'Most likely rat piss.'

Grady pressed the button on the walkie-talkie, clenched tightly in his hand like a comfort blanket, to speak to his brother.

'We're inside, and you never said anything about it stinking of rat piss.'

'What did you expect, little bro?' the amused voice came over the airwave. 'The smell of freshly mown grass and bubble gum?'

'You still could have given us the heads up.'

'And spoil the surprise? Speak to you in a bit, be safe.'

'We need to find that generator,' Ben spoke. 'From what Joey told us, there's one in this foyer.'

The beams of torchlight danced around the foyer floor wildly, landing on the occasional nonplussed rat, who refused to panic or concede ground to these strangers who had invaded their domain.

'What if there's no petrol left in the generator?' Dale enquired.

'Then we're fucked,' Grady responded with harshness.

'Not necessarily,' said Ben. 'There may still be the dynamo here, which they used for electricity back in the day.'

'Are you guys really willing to trust the electrics in this place after all these years of neglect?' Callum shot down. 'Even if they're still working, there's more than a strong chance they'll short out, or worse still, start an electrical fire.'

'Jesus, is this here termy the only optimistic one amongst you all?' Ben responded self-deprecatingly. 'I'm sure it will be fine.'

After a few more minutes of clumsy surveying in the limited darkness, like a drunkard trying to find the keyhole to the front door, Grady's torch fell upon the generator.

'Got it.'

'Moment of truth,' Dale sighed as he made his way over and leant down to inspect it. The three others all focused their lights on the generator to aid him.

'Do you even know how to work these things?' Grady challenged.

'Should be straightforward enough to figure out. Besides, I'm going to have to learn at some point for when I'm in the Engineers. What better time to start learning than now?'

The initial sound of spluttering, once the ignition chord had been pulled several times, was like that of a heavy smoker clearing his chest as he took his morning breaths, yet it soon gave way to a monotonous drone. The lights began to flicker after the initial burst of electricity began to surge and breathe life into them.

The grand hall they were standing in was a large and open space. It was rectangular-shaped and numerous closed doorways to other rooms surrounded its perimeter. At the midpoint on the lefthand side of the hall was a black, painted, iron, spiral staircase which ascended to the top floor, approximately ten metres above them.

The upstairs was of a similar layout to the downstairs, yet with a metre-wide concourse running the perimeter. There was a metre-high guardrail around the edge of this concourse. Callum couldn't help but ponder this guardrail must have been more for aesthetics rather than any practical protection of the patients who once lived here - since anyone with suicidal tendencies, and he held no doubt there would have been many who'd harboured them, would have been able to vault the rails and plummet to their deaths or serious injuries with little bother. He found himself morbidly examining the floor for any lingering stains of blood, yet he saw none, just a carpet of dust and rat shit.

The grand hall's interior walls showed the inevitable signs of cobwebs and deterioration after all these years of neglect. Most noticeable were the large patches of black mould scattered about the walls.

'That's not a good sign,' Dale spoke with seriousness as he acknowledged the black stains. 'My Grampy used to tell us that black mould patches are the traces of the wicked and wronged souls trying to make their way back into the land of the living. If you're to stare at the black mould for long and hard enough, it will drive you to madness.' There was a brief pause as he watched the others digest his words, he smiled a sly smile. 'But I wouldn't think too much on it, my Grampy was about as unhinged as an old garden gate.'

'Hey guys,' Ben's voice came as he held the Polaroid camera aloft to signal a group photograph was required. 'Time for us to be local legends.' He took a photo of Callum, Dale, and Grady.

Callum thought it might even have been a nice photo had it not been for Grady waving his middle finger at the camera. 'The camera never lies,' he thought. 'And this photo will show Grady fucking Daley being the same arsehole as always.'

Ben retrieved the photo and gently placed it in his pocket. He would look at it properly later when it had fully developed.

'Hey Grade,' he said. 'Can you take a photo of me with the others?'

'Sure thing,' Grady complied with no sign of petulance or sarcasm. Though Callum was loath to admit it, he had to concede that for all of his numerous faults, he at least appeared sincere and dedicated in his friendship with Ben.

The four of them found a patch in the centre of the hall floor where they would set up base and began to unpack their backpacks.

Dale unrolled a thick picnic blanket. Once unfurled, it was large enough for all four of them to fit on. It might not have been enough to make their sitting any more comfortable, but at least it meant they weren't sitting directly on the floor's unsanitary surface.

He then unpacked a thermos flask of tea, something Grady scoffed at as he produced several bottles of spirits he'd purchased. Some vodka, some Southern Comfort, and some Peach Schnapps which he handed to Callum. If handing over this perceived feminine drink was part of some thinly veiled dig at Callum's masculinity, then the joke was on Grady, since it was he who would have been out of pocket for buying it.

'A drink for m'lady,' he teased in a mocking gentlemanly accent. 'Are you sure you can handle taking something straight?'

'No, but ask your dad how he liked taking something bent,' Callum quipped back. This wasn't the first time he had heard such barbs, and he was sure he would hear many more in his lifetime.

Grady's face turned sour at this comeback. His eyes caught those of Dale's, who was staring at him in a manner which indicated, should he carry on his taunting of Callum, he would respond with something more than wit.

As if to salvage some sense of superiority, Grady reached into his backpack and pulled out a battery-operated FM radio and placed it on the blanket.

'It beats listening to you two waffle on all night,' he addressed Dale and Callum.

'We have plenty of time to listen to that later,' Ben spoke with excitement. 'I'm going to explore first. Coming all this way here just to sit on a blanket is the same as travelling all the way to Disney World just to stand outside the entrance.'

'I'll come with,' Grady assured. He threw Dale and Callum a look that said, "Don't worry, I'll keep an eye on him."

'You two coming?' Ben asked.

'We'll catch up with you in a bit, mucka,' Dale replied. 'We'll just finish setting up base first. Remember, we don't know how structurally sound this place is—you saw what happened to Grady on those steps outside. Slow and steady about this place, okay?'

'Yes, mum,' Ben mocked, to which he was given a high-five from Grady.

CHAPTER FOUR

Ben and Grady began to explore the grand hall with greater scrutiny now there was light. As ordered by Joseph, and also heeding Callum's words about not wanting to short the electrics, they had made sure only to have enough lights on as necessary.

Grady scraped at the thick layer of dust and dried pellets of rat droppings with one of his Doc Marten boots to reveal a patch of the marbled floor.

'This Davenport dude must have had some monster money,' he observed. 'What a waste. Do you think he'd have ever built it in the first place knowing the state it would end up in and how neglected it would be?'

'I don't think some people care about what they leave behind. You're dead far longer than you're alive. Why not make the most of the hand you've been given while you're still here?'

'Yeah, well you're not dying on me yet, you termy bastard, you've still got enough time to do shit. Hell, we're doing this tonight, ain't we? That's already more than most of the suckers in this town have done in their insignificant lives. Besides, dying young automatically makes you much more interesting than most of those who die old. When people are walking around Hulmsford cemetery in years to come, snooping at the gravestones of strangers, who do you think is going to stand out more to them? Some old fart who died at 86 years old, or some 18-year-old?'

The two of them came to one of the closed doors; a rusted brass door number was still screwed into the wooden panelling of the once-white door—it was the number 9.

Ben threw Grady a mischievous gaze that was daring him to open it.

'I didn't come here just to babysit your pasty, skinny arse,' Grady replied.

Both of them giggled as Grady placed his hand on the

brass handle.

A sudden and heavy coughing fit invaded Ben, putting a halt to both of their laughter. He placed the sleeve of the raincoat he was still wearing over his mouth to muffle the coughs. The concerned expression was evident on Grady's face.

'Hey, is everything okay over there?' Dale called out. The coughing had been loud enough to travel to his spot.

Though Ben couldn't yet find his voice, he nodded at Grady to confirm he was alright.

'Yeah, he's fine,' Grady shouted.

The lack of any subsequent barbed comment or insults suggested to Dale that Ben wasn't as okay as was being reported.

Once the coughs had stopped, Ben removed his sleeve from his mouth.

Though his coat was red, it wasn't enough to disguise the flecks of blood present. He wiped it against the side of his jacket to hide the evidence, but it was too late; Grady had already clocked onto it.

'Don't say anything,' Ben pleaded weakly. 'You know how much I need tonight.'

'You're my boy,' Grady begrudgingly submitted. 'I've got your back.' He grabbed the brass knob again and twisted it—the door was unlocked.

He pushed it open, allowing the two friends to enter.

The room was in partial darkness. The only light invading it was that which the open door allowed to enter from the hall.

With the electrics on, and the hall lit up, the two of them had neglected to bring their torches with them for this initial round of exploration—something they immediately regretted.

'I'm going to make a feel on the walls to see if there are any switches,' Grady informed.

'Try not to think about any bugs or spiders that might be on there,' Ben replied with puckishness, knowing it would be impossible for his friend not to think about those things now he had put the notion out there. Grady had let slip to him once he was scared of spiders, and Ben wasn't going to let such information go to waste.

'Arsehole. Won't you just curl up and die already?' Grady mocked.

His hand found the light switch and turned it on, allowing the room to fully reveal itself.

The room had once been painted white, though now, its brilliance had long since faded into a drab and dirty coat. The traces of black mould were present in this room too.

In the corner of the room, there was a rusted metal frame of a single-person bed. Though the mattress was still upon it, the sheets and pillows had been removed.

'They must have only taken the stuff which wasn't a ball-ache to carry or remove when it was closed down after the incident of 1917,' Ben reasoned.

'Holy shit,' Grady spoke with amazement. 'Have you seen this?'

Ben was quick to join him, his mind eager to see the first trace of evidence that gave justice to this building's reprehensible reputation.

'What are we looking at, dude?' Ben asked.

Grady pointed towards some fine claw marks on the wall, about three feet from the floor.

'Probably the rats,' Ben spoke with tones of disappointment.

'They'd have to be mammoth rats to claw that high,' Grady countered. So as to prove his point, he got down on his knees and mimicked clawing from his kneeling position at the same height as the claw marks. 'These were done by a human.'

Ben knelt beside his friend and took a photo on his Polaroid, carefully placing the still into his pocket with the others once done.

'Oh my God,' he spoke aghast. 'You're right.' He leaned in closer to the scratch marks and began to pry something away from one of the serrations with his fingernail.

'That's gross, dude,' said Grady. 'Make sure you wash your hands before you go picking your nose.'

'Got it,' Ben sighed with satisfaction as something small dropped to the floor. Ben picked up the object between his forefinger and thumb. He held it a little too close to Grady's eyes, in part to show him his discovery, but principally to gross him out. It was a fingernail, not a meagre clipping though, but the whole nail. It was thicker and longer than usual and yellowed, but it was without doubt human.

'They must have been clawing so hard, the nail came away from the finger,' Ben theorised.

'Fucking hell, put that thing down, won't you? You'll catch a disease.'

'You're right, I might die or something,' Callum quipped. His gallows humour was in full force tonight.

'Yeah, but still. Think of your immune system, dude.'

'Bloody hell, Grade, you're meant to be the fun one.'

After a few more minutes of exploring the room to see if there was anything else of grotesque note to report back to the others, the boys decided to leave the room and see what else they could find around the building.

As they tried a few more doors, they observed the other rooms were of the same setup, and most still contained the single bed frame and mattress.

'Hey, I've got an idea,' Grady declared as he opened the door to yet another unlocked room around the hall's perimeter.

As he had anticipated, it looked no different to the others - minus the human claw marks. Instead of entering the room, he turned his attention to the picnic blanket.

'Hey Dale!' he yelled. 'Can we borrow you for a few minutes?'

'Do I need to be worried about what's going on in that head of yours?' Ben questioned.

'Sweet innocent little old me? Of course not.'

Dale joined them at the doorway to the room.

'What's up?'

'Give me a hand bringing some of those mattresses out to where we're sat,' Grady ordered. 'As long as we put them back before we leave, so Joey doesn't get in any shit, they'd be far more comfortable for us to sit on than that picnic blanket.'

CHAPTER FIVE

When Dale and Grady finished bringing the fourth mattress to their spot in the hall and placed it to form a perimeter around the picnic blanket, Callum and Ben had been deep in laughter.

Although Ben's laughter was hindered by his shortness of breath and undisguisable coughs at times, it was enough to bring a contagious smile to Dale and Grady's faces too - despite not being privy to whatever conversation they were catching intermittent snippets of throughout their ferrying of the mattresses.

'Ey up fellas, what did we miss?' Dale asked.

'We were talking about Mr Hutchins, our old chemistry teacher. He'd left the school a little under a year before you'd arrived,' Callum partially elaborated.

'Bloody hell, that's a name from the past. A horrible old bastard he was too,' Grady added. 'He had all the charm of a papercut to the tongue. What happened to him that one time in assembly couldn't have happened to a nicer arsehole.'

Callum and Ben burst into another bout of laughter.

'Do you want to hear a secret?' Ben said once his laughs had subsided and he'd reclaimed much of his breath.

'How can I not want to hear it?' Grady replied. 'Asking someone if they want to hear a secret is like a diabetic being offered an extra slice of cake. You know it's not right that you have it, but how can you resist saying no?'

'Well, what happened to Mr Hutchins at the assembly, it was Callum and I who were behind it.'

'For God's sake, fellas,' Dale was starting to voice rare frustration. 'What the hell happened?'

'Callum, would you like to do the honours?' Ben spoke.

'With pleasure.

Mr Hutchins, aside from being our chemistry teacher and one of the strictest teachers in the school, was also something of a functioning alcoholic.

He tried to hide it as best as he could, and to his credit, he hid it well. Well enough from those who mattered, anyhow. The speed with which he drew his hip flask, released a shot, and placed it back in the inner pocket of his jacket would have seen him the envy of any gunslinger in the old west.

Yet, unbeknownst to Hutchins, a new sheriff was in town, Callum the Kid.

Mr Hutchins was also Ben's and my registration teacher for the year, and he used to hold morning registry in his chemistry classroom.

He was on his usual mean form that morning and had already made a few of the girls cry with one of his typically insensitive comments, and that didn't sit right with Ben and me. We knew we wanted to do something to bring him down a peg or two, but we didn't know what, and we didn't know how.

Sometimes in life, however, destiny finds a way to screw you over for cheap laughs just as much as the stars align to change the world for the betterment. This was one of those moments.

The cataclysmic chain of events had been set in motion by the headmaster calling in an emergency morning off, and in a definition of irony, the reason being was that his pet dog had eaten a load of important paperwork.

In any case, Hutchins had been called upon to take the weekly school assembly at very short notice. With approximately thirty minutes to prepare, he was taking more and more hits of his "special coffee" to calm himself.

I mean, he barely enjoyed presenting to a class of twenty, let alone a couple of hundred.

Ben and I called a secret huddle to enact our plan.

For Ben, his mission was a simple one: he would start a heated argument with one of the boys at our table, enough to provoke him into a shoving match. After all, was this not a classroom used for chemistry lessons? Even the arguments should be fully combustible.

It would result in a detention for Ben and the poor unwitting scapegoat who had inadvertently been roped into our ruse, but like any game of chess, the pawns are there to be sacrificed.

Whilst the skirmish was going on, Hutchins would have no choice but to come over and diffuse it.

With Hutchins' and the rest of the class's attention on Ben and the other lad, I was able to crawl undetected to the cupboard where some of the containers of the non-lethal chemicals were kept for the practical lessons, Polyethylene Glycol included.'

Callum noted the confusion on Dale and Grady's collective faces upon revealing the chemical's name.

'Polyethylene Glycol,' Callum repeated as if it would make any difference. 'Something that is known to have a strong laxative effect. Now, I had no idea how much to put into Hutchins' coffee or how quickly it would take effect, so I gambled on a third of the bottle before I snuck back to the desk.

Registration had finished and it was time for the weekly school assembly.

Hutchins was showing no signs of the effects of the Polyethylene, and Ben and I had resigned ourselves that our little gambit had been unsuccessful. As it turned out, however, it had worked better than we could ever have realised.

Hutchins had been mid-speech, trying to shoehorn some topical news story from the night before into it whilst attempting to spin it into some analogy about it fitting into the school's ethos.

Most of the pupils listening to his meandering monologue had already drifted off and were daydreaming about whatever it was we used to daydream about at that age, when suddenly everyone's attention was brought back to the room by an almighty squelching sound churning around in Hutchins' stomach.

Ben and I threw a look at each other as we anticipated what was about to go down. For Mr Hutchins though, his realisation came too late. It wasn't so much of a Code Red for him to hurry off the stage but a Code Brown.

Unfortunately for him, that poor, miserable bastard didn't make it in time.'

'Holy shit,' Dale proclaimed.

'More like a whole load of shit,' Ben quipped.

'So, what happened to him after that? I don't think I'd ever be able to show my face again,' asked Dale.

'Neither did he,' said Ben. 'He never came back to Hulmsford Comprehensive after the incident. As far as we know, he took up a teaching job somewhere else in Hertfordshire. All we do know for sure is none of the pupils at Hulmsford were sorry to see him go, and it was a fitting end to such a shitty person.'

'I saw him once after that,' Callum stated. 'I was walking to school by myself and was running late for morning bell.

He was standing outside the school in that same shirt and tie he always used to wear. He didn't look well at all. His eyes were bloodshot, and he wasn't clean-shaven. Looking at him, it was clear he'd been drinking heavily.

We ended up catching each other's eye line, but he didn't say anything to me, he simply stared at me with that same old mean look he used to give the rest of the pupils.

There was something about his look this time though which was different. Usually, that look of his would intimidate me, but this one, I don't know. It made me feel so, well, frightened. I can't explain how or why. It just really unnerved me.'

'Well fuck that guy,' said Grady as he gave Callum a surprisingly affectionate slap upon his back.

'So, shall we go explore some more?' Ben asked excitedly once silence had fully returned to their group.

'What's the rush, eager beaver?' Dale spoke. 'We've got all night for that. I'm going to have a drink and a chill for a bit first.'

'I've also brought some weed if you want some,' Grady offered.

'I best not,' Dale answered. 'That stuff stays in the system for a couple of weeks, and I don't want to take the gamble on having a couple of days getting beasted by the regiment police if they piss-test me when I get to the army base.'

'Fair enough, I guess. How about you, evil genius? You're off to university in a few weeks, aincha? Getting stoned is part of every respectable student's curriculum. And don't give me some bullshit about it killing off your brain cells, you've got more than enough to spare. Besides, I don't hand out my pot for free to anyone, that is unless they're OK in my books.'

Callum smiled and took the pre-rolled joint from Grady; it was the closest thing he anticipated to an olive branch or, in this case, a peace pipe, from his habitual tormentor - and all it took was making a former teacher shit themselves to get it.

'And for you, Termy, an extra strong one—for medicinal purposes, of course.' Grady pulled out an extra-large, almost comically-sized joint from his backpack.

'So, what now?' Ben asked as Grady lit the joint for him.

'Isn't it tradition to tell spooky stories in situations such as these?' Dale stated.

The other three nodded their agreement.

'A story about this place?' Grady suggested.

'Nah, we already know pretty much every story there is about this place thanks to Ben here,' Dale spoke. 'How about something new? Cal, you're always quick at coming up with a story or two, how about it?'

Callum smiled.

'Well, there is one I've been working on as part of a going-away present for Private Reeves here. It only seems fitting it's a story set in the army. It's called, "The Chamber".'

Even though the Sgt's Mess was quiet that night, Sergeant Jeffrey Sherring—Sherry to his friends—elected to sit in the corner of the large bar room, purposely keeping himself in the shadows so as not to be bothered. There was only one person he wanted to liaise with this evening, and he was already running late.

The reason for Sgt Eddie "Hoppo" Hopkins' lateness was evident as he took his seat opposite Sherry at the small round table with his pint of bitter. The lingering scent of perfume was harder to hide than the flushed look upon his face.

'Sorry I'm late, Sherry. I had a prior affair to deal with.'

'So it would seem,' came the sardonic reply. 'What was her name?'

'Now, now. A gentleman never tells.'

'Firstly, you may be many things, Hoppo, but a gentleman, alas, is not one of them. Secondly, whatever piece of crumpet you're shagging is none of my business. You know full well why I asked you here tonight.'

Hopkins rolled his eyes. He at least wanted to enjoy his pint before the atmosphere was sullied. He took a hefty gulp of his beer to savour as much of it as he could untainted before hearing the name of his nemesis. He hadn't even succeeded in placing the glass back on the Albright beer mat before it was spoken.

'Giles,' Sherring spoke with disdain.

Hopkins let out a sigh of solidarity.

'You had him for field exercises today, right?' Hopkins stated.

'And don't I know it. You have no idea what the cockwomble did this time. Even by his impeccably low standards of common sense or intellect, this was a whole new level of dumbfuckery.'

Hopkins' mind began to work overtime as to what depths of stupidity Private Duncan Giles had managed to achieve this time.

The Giles to whom they were referring was five weeks into his ten weeks' basic training for the Fusiliers and was proving to be such an unmitigated disaster, he made Sgt

Bilko look like Rambo in comparison.

He was such a perpetual daydreamer, even when it came to the simplest of commands, he would find a medley of ways to screw up.

Hell, he couldn't even manage to march in time, and the only thing he had perfected on the Parade Square was the dubious art of Tik-Toking—marching with the same side arm and leg at the same time.

Sherring and Hopkins weren't concerned at first. They'd had at least one person like Giles in every intake they had been delegated to instruct in Field Lessons—the bread and butter of every new soldier.

At first, they took occasional amusement in his inadvertent antics, giving them the perfect opportunity to try out their latest material of berating insults aimed at the recruits.

Yet, these tirades were water off a duck's back when it came to Giles. Half the time, they wondered if their verbal affronts were being listened to at all.

Then came the beastings, the physical punishments dished out for not doing what was ordered, or to the standard expected.

During their long service, they had seen many a potential soldier quit over the intensity of the physicality, seeing mighty oaks of men reduced to tears and feeling like delicate saplings. Yet, no matter how many beastings they bestowed upon Giles, he seemed impervious to the physical ordeals. It would have been impressive to them had it not been so infuriating.

As measures of desperation, they had even taken the soft and delicate approach which defied their very nature as field instructors. Asking with sugar-coated TLC if he was sure this was the career he wanted. 'After all,' as they put it to him, 'someone with your characteristics and fortitude would thrive out on Civvie Street.'

Unsurprisingly, however, their words went in through one ear and out of the other, not even stopping en route to take in their clearly hollow surroundings.

At first, the instructors' frustrations over their failings at making this screw-up anything remotely close to being a competent soldier were due to the dangers this recruit would pose to his brothers-in-arms should he ever be in a real-life battle zone—and God forbid, carrying live ammo. He would be a hazard to comrades and civilians alike.

As the weeks went on, however, their frustrations over their failings had become just as much a matter of pride. Somehow their teachings were seeing him become even less capable.

'Go on, Sherry,' Hopkins sighed. 'What's the wankpuffin done now?'

'We were doing some formation training out in the woods, and I said for the squad to pair up, and whilst one of them moves between the trees, the other one covers him.'

'Riiight,' Hopkins said with uncertainty. He wasn't quite sure where this anecdote was heading.

'Well, whilst that fucktard Giles' partner, Donaldson, was running between the trees, Giles was chasing him throwing all kinds of leaves and twigs on him.'

Hopkins could only shake his head with bemusement.

'I shouted out to him, "Giles, you nobweasel, what on earth are you doing?" "I'm covering him, Sergeant," he replied, as if it was me who was the fucking idiot for asking. I yelled at him, "Cover him with your fucking rifle, you dumb piece of shit!" Do you know what his response was?'

'Not that fucking look he does.'

'That fucking look he does. That stupid simpleton smile, as if I'd just told him a joke that he didn't quite get but thought it best to smile anyway so as not to hurt my feelings.'

'I'm telling you, Sherry, he's going to get someone killed before basic training's over.'

'I know.' Sherring's voice was more hushed now. 'Which is why I wanted to talk to you here tonight. This conversation goes no further than the two of us, understand?'

'Yeah, of course, you can trust me, Sherry.'

'That's what I thought. So, it's the chamber for his squad next week, as you know.'

Hopkins nodded his head. He thought about mimicking Giles's simpleton look to mess with Sherring a little, but it was clear to him he was hot under the collar right now and Sherring had been known to let fly with a fist from time to time when his fuse was burnt too short. He had even been through mandatory counselling for his temper to avoid facing a court-martial for punching a recruit whilst instructing them. One more strike, no pun intended, and he would likely be kicked out to Civvie Street via a short stint in a military cell.

Hoppo had to concede that this therapy appeared to be working; it had to have been, how else had he avoided punching Giles so far?

'So, you thinking about giving him some extra attention in the chamber?' Hopkins asked.

The CS gas chamber to which he was referring was a mandatory part of the recruits' basic training. They would be required to line up inside the chamber whilst wearing their NBC (Nuclear Biological Chemical) suits and respirator, then one by one remove their respirator to become briefly exposed to the CS gas—a powerful and temporarily debilitating form of tear gas.

'To what end?' Sherring sighed. 'The effects are short term. Sure, giving him a bit of extra exposure to the tear gas may make him suffer for a while longer, but ten minutes later, he'll just be back to being his usual maddening self. I wouldn't even be surprised if he gives us that same simpleton look while he's being gassed.'

'So, what are you suggesting?'

'Something that could be the end of both our careers if we get found out.' Sherring could see Hoppo was looking a bit uncomfortable at hearing this. 'Listen, it's all or nothing,' Sherry continued. 'I know it's a massive risk but so is having him get to finish basic training and pass out. I know I'm willing to risk my career to know my fellow servicemen will be that much safer.'

'Okay, I'll hear you out.'

Sherry smiled a soft, nervous smile. He looked around the mess to ensure they were still alone, or at the least, not in danger of being overheard.

'I've got a friend, who to protect both you, and him, shall remain nameless. Anyway, this friend works in the development of some of the more, shall we say, experimental weapons for the army. Those not yet approved.

The department is close to finalising a new type of experimental non-lethal gas. Whereas CS gas debilitates you physically, this one fucks with your mind.

The way my friend pitched it, it's the worst trip you'll ever go on for a couple of hours, it's not so much LSD but HelLSD.'

He can get me a canister of this stuff in time for next week, all hush-hush of course. You know how they work in those departments—it will help them with the testing of a live subject for the product – unofficially, of course.

All we need to do is keep Giles back until last, wait until all the other privates are out of the chamber, then we switch canisters.'

'And you think this will work?'

'I do. If anyone asks any questions as to why he's freaking out so badly, we just say he had a bad mental reaction to the CS. No one's going to question it's my contact's experimental gas because, quite frankly, no one in our base knows of its existence yet. We may even be able to spin it so people think he's taken some drugs or something—that alone should be grounds for an unconditional discharge. Either way, that twatbadger will get what's coming to him.'

Hoppo took another swig of his beer.

'I'll need to think about it.'

'You've got less than a week before the chamber, and our chance to get him out of here.'

The following week for Hopkins passed with seemingly great speed. Any reservations he may have held over the chamber plan had been chipped away with a sledgehammer by Giles' continued stupidity and recklessness. The most flabbergasting of which had been on the rifle range.

It wasn't so much Giles' erratic grouping of the live rounds on his target, or the fact he wasn't listening to Hopkins' instructions on how to improve his accuracy—it had been the blatant disregard for safety on the range.

It had been instructed far too many times already to the recruits that they should keep their rifles pointed at the targets on the range at all times, yet when Hopkins addressed Giles to focus on his breathing between shots, he had instinctively turned around to face his instructor, rifle and all.

Seeing that simpleton smile whilst having a loaded rifle pointed at him was enough to cause rare panic in Hopkins. What if his finger had twitched? What if it had been another recruit he had been pointing at?

That little stunt had seen Giles receive the beasting of all beastings, yet as per usual, it was water off a duck's back. That was the moment Hopkins knew he was all in on Sherring's plan.

Inside the CS Chamber, Sherring and Hopkins had manufactured it so Giles would be the last in the line to be exposed to the CS gas. It didn't take much for the rest of the squad to realise the reasons why—the field instructors were going to fuck with him and then some. The fellow privates had already started sledging Giles over this, and Sherring and Hopkins could already picture his trademark simpleton look underneath the respirator in response.

Before the recruits began their exposure to the CS gas, they were subjected en masse to a brief bit of exercise, though inside those thick and heavy NBC suits and respirator, any form of exercise would be considered a beating.

Several concentrated minutes of press-ups, squats and burpees was the order of the day. Unsurprisingly, Giles had fastened up the bottoms to his NBC suit incorrectly, and upon completion of his first burpee, they had fallen around his ankles, earning him yet another berating from his instructors.

With the physical foreplay over, it was now time for the main event. A canister of the strong tear gas was released into the chamber.

The exercise was simple: the recruit was to inhale a deep breath, remove the respirator, then recite their rank, name, service number, the name of their squadron and their field instructor. It took several seconds for the effects of the gas to hit them, and, depending on their tolerance to this gas, midway through reciting their statement, the debilitating stinging would begin.

Depending on the mood of their instructor, the recruits would be allowed to exit the chamber immediately upon completing the information or asked another couple of questions, purely for shits and giggles. More often than not, it was the latter.

There were, inevitably, a few minor mishaps present. One recruit had foolishly taken off his respirator before taking the big inhale of breath, meaning the effects were almost instantaneous, and no statement came close to being completed.

Another had forgotten to collect his helmet, which he had taken off during the burpees, and had to navigate the room despite the stinging of his eyes and lungs to find his misplaced helmet.

Then it was time for Giles.

Hopkins reached into the bag of canisters and retrieved the only one with a flash of red tape across the label. He performed a subtle nod to Sherring. There were just the three of them in the chamber now. They let loose with the canister; there was no going back.

Giles took his deep breath and removed his respirator. He hadn't even made it past reciting his service number by the time the flash of fear made its way into his watery eyes.

The respirator masks of his two instructors began to turn to flesh, though still maintaining the same shape and design. They then began clawing at this new nightmarish skin, raking away at it, frantically and deeply. Through the chasms of the claw marks, a swarm of large, maggot-like creatures found their way to the surface, making their presence known.

The frightened scream came from Giles as the parasites dropped from the facial wounds onto the floor of the chamber and slithered their way with surprising speed towards him.

Giles took a panicked step backwards, though to what end? All he had succeeded in doing was backing himself into a wall. He had trapped himself.

The two figures began grabbing fistfuls of these parasitic creatures from their wounds, pulling clumps of their shredded flesh with them. They hurled these parasites at Giles, laughing maniacally as they did so.

Giles' screams became more frantic now as he caught a closer look at the parasites that had been thrown onto him. They were like no maggots he had seen before. These had jagged rows of teeth.

Though the NBC suit was resistant against chemicals and gases, it was not impervious to the gnawing of these larvae who were burrowing through the suit and through his flesh. It was Giles now who was clawing at his skin to get these creatures off him.

Though this act of self-mutilation was a hallucination, his screams were real. The pain he felt was real.

'Please, make it stop,' he whimpered in horror.

'Maybe we should get him out of here now,' Hopkins uttered to Sherring.

'Thirty more seconds,' the cold reply came.

Giles couldn't even complete his screams now due to the

debilitating effects of the HelLSD. Every time he opened his mouth to scream, more of these maggoty creatures entered through this opening. They were inside him now. Feeding on his insides, feeding on his brain.

'Get him out of here, now,' Hopkins shouted again. He had no love lost for the recruit, but even he was feeling sorry for him and whatever it was he was witnessing.

'Ten more seconds,' Sherring defied.

Giles began headbutting the wall of the chamber hard. It was the only way he could think of to swat these creatures who were tunnelling inside his brain. This act of self-harm was no hallucination.

This was enough for Sherring to get him out of there in haste. There could be no signs of physical abuse that could be traced back to him or Hopkins should any questions be asked.

Sherring opened the door to the chamber and Giles sprinted out screaming.

The fresh air reacting to the remnants of the gas in the pores of his skin only served to cause more irritation to Giles, yet the recruit mistook this for more of these creatures attaching themselves to him.

He continued his cries of despair as he grabbed his helmet and smashed it into his face in an attempt to fight the parasites that only he could see.

It took two of his fellow recruits to restrain him from causing any more damage to himself. Though there would likely be heavy swelling, he appeared not to have broken any bones of his skull.

Sherring and Hopkins exited the chamber and removed their respirators, the look of concern present on both their faces.

'He must have had a bad neurological reaction to the gas,' he reasoned to the squad looking at them aghast with concern and curiosity. 'Anyone would swear he was on drugs,' he then spoke almost as an afterthought, suddenly remembering this had been part of the plan all along, though maybe not as intense.

It was a claim they repeated to their commanding officer when they were debriefing him on the events and why one of their recruits had appeared to have a complete mental and physical breakdown in the chamber.

'Well, we'll be sure to get him blood and urine tested to see if that's the case, gentlemen,' their officer responded. 'If there are any traces of drugs in his system, we'll be sure to take disciplinary action accordingly. Until he calms down though, he's going to be placed on medical supervision in any instance. Though it could be argued that he was never wired correctly in the first place, it would be fair to say, at the moment, those wires aren't even connected to anything at all.'

Three days passed. Three gloriously Giles-free days. Their plan, it would seem, had been a successful one. Then, that morning, as they prepared to take their squad to the rifle range, they saw Giles lining up with the others. If there was any consolation to them, his simpleton smile had all but gone; it appeared that any expression upon his face had disappeared altogether. Just as before, he still looked to be in his own little world, yet unlike before, he didn't appear to be daydreaming—he didn't appear to be contemplating anything at all.

Sherring threw a subtle look to Hopkins that suggested he was unsure what to do about the situation. A look that Hoppo returned in kind. Nonetheless, he barked the orders at the squad to commence their march to the range.

'How's our degenerate doing?' Hopkins asked Sherring as they congregated on the range after completing a sweep of supervising the recruits' efforts.

'The most remarkable thing,' Sherring replied. 'I'm not saying he's going to get singled out as a future sniper or anything, but his accuracy and grouping has improved drastically.'

'Well, let's not go counting our blessings yet. I'm not convinced he's fit enough to be out here. You've seen the look on him—those lights may be on, but no fucker is in there.'

'Maybe, but they wouldn't have released him from the medical bay had they any concerns. Hang back by here and supervise the rest of the recruits. I'm going to go over and talk to him, see if I can get anything out of him over how he's doing.'

'Hold your fire!' Sherring bellowed to the squad.

Hopkins nodded his head as he observed the sergeant make his way over to Giles, who was lying down in the shooting position. He watched Sherring kneel beside him, lift the right cup of his ear defenders and say something.

Though Hoppo wasn't privy to what was being said, he'd had an awful feeling about it nonetheless. There was a look of satisfaction on Sherring when he addressed their mutual nemesis.

Hoppo watched the sergeant make his way back over, the same look of satisfaction etched upon him. Sherring took his place a few metres to his side.

'What did you say to him?' Hopkins asked. His unease over the situation was proving too much for him to resist.

'I told him it was you who did this to him in the chamber.'

Before Hopkins could analyse the statement, he was distracted by the sound of shocked gasps from some of the recruits. Giles had stood up and was pointing the rifle in their direction, the look of pure hatred upon his face. He let off two shots. The first hit Hopkins in the gut, the second on himself as he placed the weapon under his chin and pressed the trigger.

Sherring was the first to reach the wounded Sergeant, the amount of blood pouring out of him indicated he wouldn't survive long enough for any medics to get to him.

'Why?' Hopkins spluttered, the life rapidly draining from him.

'Do you really think I didn't know about you and my wife?' the cold response came. 'I've been smelling her brand of perfume lingering on you for months now. My anger therapy has been good for me—it's taught me revenge is so much more rewarding when you have patience.'

Sherring adopted a mocking version of the same simpleton look Giles used to display. The look Hopkins hated so much. It would be the last thing he would see.

CHAPTER SIX

'Er, thank you,' Dale spoke once Callum finished. 'For that unnecessarily dark leaving gift.'

Callum returned a smile to him which said, 'You're welcome.'

'I hope you're a better recruit than that Giles fuckwit,' Grady laughed.

'You'll be fine,' Callum added. 'I've no doubt you'll thrive in the Forces. Either way, I'm going to miss you, my friend.'

'Let's nip this soppy shit in the bud before things get too sentimental,' Ben intervened as he briefly checked his wristwatch. 'What say you put some tunes on, Grade?'

Grady picked up his portable radio as if he was a jealous partner, and no one was to touch his love other than himself. He turned it on and placed it back down in the centre of the boys.

The station he had set it to was Herts and Soul AM, a local broadcaster based in Hertfordshire County. Though its various disc jockeys could only be described as enthusiastic at best, they often made up for their evident amateurism with their savvy playlists.

Upon recognising the station, a beaming smile found itself upon Dale's face.

It wasn't so much the station itself that brought him great comfort in this most discomforting of surroundings, but the show currently broadcasting.

It was the Swinging Sixties Hour, hosted by DJ Rebel Ian—an alter ego bordering on violating the Trade Descriptions Act, since nothing about him screamed rebellious at all. Even if this middle-aged, middle-class disc jockey were to cause havoc, most of Hertfordshire would be too asleep to take notice anyway, what with him having been relegated to the 01:00 shift of the programming.

Dale's love of this era of music had come from his father and the extensive 45 rpm record collection which had been acquired by him.

Growing up, Dale's family never experienced much in the way of financial stability. His mother had never been able to work anything other than part-time hours due to her chronic arthritis, despite not yet reaching middle age, and his father mustered only occasional employment.

As a result, whilst the rest of the world was becoming increasingly familiar with colour televisions and video recorders in their homes, the Reeves were still playing catch-up with their portable black and white. As for VHS, or even a second-hand Betamax, that was nothing but a pipe dream.

Their financial situation had started to become more stable, however, when Malcolm Reeves had been able to hold down employment as an overnight delivery driver for a hospitality chain.

Though this job paid far from a king's ransom, it at least meant things were at long last looking up for the family.

As well as the newfound financial security, another perk of Malcolm's newfound profession meant he would often return with a backpack full of 45s—from 1960s Motown to rock 'n' roll, and everything in between.

One of the delivery contracts of Malcolm's employers consisted of dropping off shipments of records to various bars and cafés for their jukeboxes. As such, the proprietors of these joints frequently gave him first choice over the waste bin for the old and seldom-played stock they were replacing.

When Dale was casually informed by his father about some of the freebies he had chosen to turn down, he was particularly vocal about his disapproval. 'Who wants Rolling Stones' "Gimme Shelter" when you can have "Fame" by Irene Cara?' Dale had naïvely challenged.

As far as his father was concerned, Dale may as well have cussed the most extreme of expletives in front of him, and for this blatant vulgarity, he would need to be educated, like a kid being forced to wash his potty mouth out with soapy water.

His father would spend much of the weekend playing the newly acquired records for Dale, B-sides included—giving him a brief history lesson into each band or artist as he did so. It sure as heck beat the history classes in school, and it sure as shit beat doing the homework he would have been made to do otherwise.

It didn't take long for Dale to concede defeat that his father had made the right choices with what records he had brought home in his quarry.

Then, one night, tragedy came—and not the Bee Gees record. A mechanical failure of his delivery truck had seen Dale's father not only lose control of his vehicle but his life as well.

The swinging sounds of the sixties which had once brought so much joy to the Reeves' household now only brought Dale's mother an all-too-heartbreaking reminder of the love she would never be able to hold again. As such, the records were donated to a charity shop, and using the out-of-court payout from Malcolm's employers, she purchased a home in Hulmsford.

She didn't know why she chose this small town specifically. She only knew she was looking for a place far from where they were currently located, and the way she saw it, if you were going to make a fresh start in your life, why not do it somewhere you have no connection or ties?

Though Dale didn't agree with his mother's shutting herself off from everything that reminded her of his father, he loved her enough to respect her wishes and not cause her any kickback or conflicts over it.

That was when he found Hearts and Soul.

Unable to sleep and suffering from night terrors—something he had kept from his mother since many of his nightmares revolved around his father, the worst of which was seeing his father's face infused onto the torso of that hideous creature from Biggsy's tale—he had taken to listening to the radio during these late hours with headphones in the jack.

He had been turning the radio dial in search of something easy to listen to when he'd landed upon the Swinging Sixties programme. Two hours of songs which were comforting and familiar to him. Records he had listened to with his father many times over. He even found therapy in pretending he was listening to them with his father again. The night terrors had stopped, and it had become his comforting nightly routine.

For Dale, sharing this moment of listening to the Swinging Sixties Programme in Davenport Manor with Ben and Callum seemed fitting.

He had already said goodbye to his father from his life, and soon he would be saying goodbye to his two best friends.

Sure, he held no doubt he would still meet up with Callum from time to time, when their service leave and term-time schedules coincided, but he was sure their best intentions to catch up with each other would erode to a matter of convenience rather than desire as the years passed.

And then there was Ben. Would he ever see him alive again after he left for his basic training? He had discussed with him about delaying his enlisting date until, well, after he'd passed, but Ben told him in no uncertain terms, and taking a phrase direct from Dale himself, 'not to be such a wazzock.'

'You'd have already passed out before I pass away,' he quipped.

'I just don't want you to not have your friends around you when you do,' his more solemn reply came.

'What sort of friend would I be if I didn't tell you to go fuck yourself? My dying wish is for you to be making the most of your life instead of worrying about mine. Promise me.'

It was an oath he was going to begrudgingly honour. At least Ben wouldn't be without a friend when that time would inevitably come. It would seem Guardian Angels came in all shapes and forms, even a Grady fucking Daley shaped one.

And though Dale still couldn't figure out why those two had connected with each other so well, he had to be grateful that they had.

Dale took a generous swig from the bottle of Southern Comfort. The warmth of the spirit was well-received in the bitterness of the autumn night, yet he was still not accustomed to the drink enough not to grimace as the burn slid down his throat. Then the station played it. His song. His father's song. 'We've Gotta Get Out of This Place' by The Animals.

A smile entered his face. He didn't need to tell Ben and Callum this was his favourite song—they already knew. Instead, they smiled with him.

It was Grady who surprised him the most as he began to mimic the iconic bass line. Callum then began to sing along, Ben too, as best he could—though without the same gusto. Dale felt duty-bound to join in. At one point, Grady had even pressed the button on the walkie-talkie for Joseph to sing in with the chorus over the channel.

For a short moment, Dale pretended his father was with him again, singing along with them too. It was all he could do not to shed a tear.

The song wound down, and as was customary for the radio DJs in order to frustrate those wanting to freeload their tracks by recording them onto cassette, he spoke over the outro in his overzealous, unnaturally cheesy DJ voice—it must have been hell for any of his listeners who were lactose intolerant.

'That was The Animals with "We've Gotta Get Out of This Place", and that song is dedicated to Dale Reeves who is about to join the Royal Engineers and is from your friends until the end, Callum and Ben.'

Dale looked over to the two of them with a beaming shit-eating smile.

'Thanks both. It means the world.'

'Thank Grady too,' Ben spoke. 'It was his idea to give you a shout-out on your favourite radio show before you left. We just did the rest.'

Grady threw a subtle nod which said, 'don't make a big deal out of it.' Dale returned the nonchalant gesture.

'Can we please go and check out upstairs now?' Ben pleaded.

'Fuck it, let's do it,' Grady replied. 'Cal, Private Reeves, you coming with us this time, or going to sit here like a couple of chickenshits?'

Dale forced himself to his feet and extended his hand out to Callum so he could pull him up.

The four of them began to make their way up the steel spiral stairs. Ben took the lead and bounded up them with excitement. He was already halfway up the staircase by the time Callum, who was leading the other two, reached the first step.

'Hey dude,' Callum shouted after him. 'Be careful, bud. You saw what happened to Grady on those steps outside. We don't know how rusted this staircase is.'

'For God's sake, Cal, you've got more whine coming out of you today than a French vineyard,' Ben retorted. 'It's fine.' To reiterate his point, Ben started jumping up and down on the step he was on. Even Grady failed to see the funny side to this. 'Come on guys, last one up has to lick a wall.'

Dale was the last one up the stairs, though the stern expression on his face suggested there was no chance in hell he was going to abide by Ben's edict that he had to lick a wall, nor was the look on his face one which said they could make him.

The first few rooms they peered into showed little difference to those on the ground level. The rooms were painted white and again possessed nothing in them other than cobwebs, an unhealthy amount of black mould, and a solitary bedframe and mattress. Thus far, aside from the grotty fingernail, the house was proving to be anticlimactic with nothing to vindicate the notoriety surrounding it. Then came an excited squeal from Ben, who had gone ahead to the next room.

'Guys! You need to look at this.'

The others joined him with haste inside the adjacent room.

Again, the layout was the same as the others: the room was off-colour white, with a bedframe and mattress within. Yet on the walls, aside from the ever-present black mould and cobwebs, there was something visibly striking and unnerving which set it apart from those they had seen thus far.

In tall lettering, on the left-hand side wall, were the words, 'No Hope.' This alone may not have been too disconcerting, yet it was the manner in which these letters were written that sent unease and disgust through each of them.

The first four letters, upon closer scrutiny, had been written in excrement by a finger.

As the realisation dawned upon them that this was no paint or crayon which had been used, a synchronised response of 'eww' escaped from the boys' mouths.

This reaction was soon snuffed into silence as they recognised what the last two letters had been written in, perhaps due to the message's author not having enough shit to finish the job. It was blood.

Ben took a photograph of the evidence and placed it with the others. With no pun intended, it was developing into one hell of a collection.

An excited smile was engraved upon his drawn-out and pale face, making him resemble the titular character from the 1928 gothic silent movie, The Man Who Laughs. Unlike that character, however, his beaming smile was only temporary; it had been dislodged by Callum as he began to rationalise the sinister message.

'Poor bastard,' he spoke in a condescending tone which evoked little sympathy for whom he was referring to. 'This would have been one of the officers from World War One when this place was being used to treat them and get their heads screwed back on straight.'

'Clearly they didn't do a good job of it,' Dale said.

'Of course they didn't. How could they?' Callum replied. 'Using this place for therapy treatment for the traumatised and shell-shocked was about as likely to be as much of a success as a sailor using a cinder block as a lifejacket. Once word got out to the patients about this place's history, along with the group trauma enabling each other, it would only have encouraged hysteria, delusion and, ultimately, violence.'

'I wonder if the guy who wrote this is the same guy who killed his fellow patients,' Grady pondered. 'I mean, it's not something a sane guy would do, right?'

'Maybe, but I guess we'll never know,' Callum replied. 'Stuff like that I imagine would be classified following the investigation, what with it being a military hospital.'

'Come on,' Ben spoke with less enthusiasm than when he had called the others into the room. 'Let's explore what else is up here.'

A couple of doors along, they came to a room which bore the number 42. Unlike the other rooms they had so far tried, this door had been locked.

Though Grady didn't say it aloud, he was grateful for this as he twisted the brass doorknob to no avail.

He would never consider himself the spiritual sort, yet the deleterious vibes he was getting from this room overwhelmed him.

The memory of every bad thing he'd ever done or said so far in his young life, of which he regretted were many, came to the forefront of his mind in one toxic tsunami. A hand grenade of negativity and remorse had detonated in his soul, almost causing him to pass out. His legs were weakened as a consequence—like they were no longer there to support him.

He disguised this sensation as best he could to the others by making out he was putting all of his weight behind the door by leaning on it to force it open. He was almost certain he had gotten away with his ruse.

For validation he wasn't alone with this sorrowful sensation, he looked over to the others to see if they were experiencing the same sensations. They too were quiet, morose even. It was scant comfort to him after all.

The silence lingered more than Grady would have liked; he wanted someone to say something, anything.

'Shall we go back downstairs?' Dale eventually spoke. The tone in which he delivered these words made the others uncertain whether it was a question or an order. Nonetheless, they all nodded in agreement and made their way back down to the ground level.

CHAPTER SEVEN

Once they were back on the ground level, they resumed their adopted positions on the mattresses.

'Did you guys feel that up there?' Ben spoke with wonderment.

'Meh,' Callum negated.

'What do you mean, meh? You were as quiet as the rest of us. Hell, you were almost as pale as me, and I've got a complexion that makes an albino look like he's spent a week in the Tropics.'

'I'll concede, I did feel something,' said Callum. 'I'm not going to deny that, but it was just the power of suggestion, beholden to the tales of this place, making us experience something that isn't. That's all.'

'That's bullshit, and you know it,' Ben argued back with a passion which was undone by the heavy cough that followed.

'Calm yourself down, dude.'

'Don't tell me to calm down. Don't you ever dare tell me that. I've earned my right to be pissed off, and then some.'

'You have, but don't get pissed off at the wrong things or people; it only leads to bitterness, and you're not that person. I've always been straight with you.'

Grady couldn't help but let out a snigger at this comment despite himself. He held up his hands to apologise straight away, yet he knew it was an empty gesture. He may not have said the words, 'Straight! First time for everything,' but his reaction had already projected the notion into the room. Even when he wasn't saying anything, he still couldn't stop being Grady fucking Daley.

'So, you haven't seen anything here that will convince you there's something unnatural here?' Ben persisted.

'Unpleasant, yes. Unsanitary, for sure. But unnatural, no. I've yet to witness anything that can't be explained by logic, science or reason.'

Callum was failing to read the infuriated expression still present on Ben's face indicating that he wanted him to stop talking for a while. He instead continued with his rationalising of everything they had experienced here so far.

'The fingernail found in the claw marks is textbook of someone suffering psychological trauma. Self-harm, alas, is an unfortunate trait. Now, I'm no expert on the subject—'

'Sure sounds like you're making yourself come off as one,' Ben mumbled to himself sourly.

Even had Callum heard this barb, he didn't show any sign of acknowledging or digesting it; he was far too busy sharing his prognosis.

'But I'm pretty certain the patients here wouldn't have had any access to anything that would facilitate them physically abusing themselves in their rooms, and this would have been their way to satisfy these harmful needs. There's a fine line between creative and primal, and sometimes those things just align. As for the No Hope message, I've already spoken my piece on the writing in blood and excrement. Which leaves us to the locked room, 42. Well, that's mostly our own doing over what we thought we experienced. Our minds aren't being aided by the pot we've smoked, or the booze we've drunk, both of which are well-known for producing side effects of paranoia. All that's happened is we've found a room we can't see inside, and our brains, knowing the supernatural stories of this place, have immediately made us think something heinous is in there. Our imaginations are always far worse than our realisations. Long story short, there is nothing here to suggest the existence of ghosts that would change my mind.'

Ben stood to his feet; tears were in his eyes now.

'I'm going to look in some more of the rooms,' he spoke, unable to hide the wavering tones in his voice. He stormed off towards the far end of the grand hall.

'I'll go keep an eye on him,' said Dale.

Callum looked towards Grady as if to ask, 'What did I say?' The look of anger returned to him said, 'Fucking everything.'

'I don't get it,' Callum sighed as if he was the blighted party.

'You really don't, do you?' The bitter rebuttal in Grady's tone landed a blow to Callum far harder than the physical ones he had dealt him with too much regularity. 'All this time, before tonight, I've hated you.'

His words were spoken with more guilt and shame than any mocking.

'It was never hatred over whether you were gay or not. The God's honest truth is shit like that has never bothered me. When that bombshell about your sexuality got out, all it was to me was a convenient smokescreen. The thing I've found about insults and bigotry is that when the target's so fucking obvious, no one actually thinks to stop and ask why you're trying to hit it in the first place.

I always hated you because of how smart you are. Let's face it, you've never had to work hard for the opportunities people like me will never get. I mean, Jesus Christ, you're even getting paid to go to that fancy university which always does the boat race thing every year. The only thing that ever came easy to me was being an arsehole.

I'm trying hard to be a better person, I swear I am, but sometimes I ask myself, why bother? The people around this shithole town don't expect me to amount to anything, so the way I see it, why work hard to meet those expectations when I can just as easily do that by doing nothing but being me?

I hate who I am most days, and I hate what I've done to people, none more so than to you—and that's the truth. I'm not going to sit here and ask for your forgiveness because I know I don't deserve it; and that's my cross to bear.'

Grady's voice had begun to break, and Callum could see the tears forming in his eyes. He wiped them away with his sleeve, not attempting to disguise them.

'My point here is,' he continued, 'having spent time with you tonight and got to know you, I've come to see now my resentment over you was misplaced. For all your big words, your articulate speaking, your facts and analysis, your need to be right all the time, you're a duffer too. The only difference is, you're as fucking dumb at reading people as I am at reading books.

It also turns out you're just as much an arsehole without trying as I am too. You've been delivering a battering to that poor bastard tonight, as bad as the ones I gave to you over the years, maybe worse. The only difference is you can't even see it.

I think the reason you took everything I threw at you and never showed signs of breaking, at least not on the outside, was because you knew you had your whole life ahead of you. Like a prisoner seeing out his sentence, all you had to do was bide your time in the knowledge that every day which passed was another day closer until you were free of this place and your fresh start.

What the hell is Ben one day closer to? An early grave, that's all. What's he got to look forward to? What fresh start can he have? Well, this place can show him hope of one.

You may think he's gone through all of his treatments already, but this is his final one. If this place can show him any sign at all of proof of the afterlife, then he will have hope his death won't truly be the end of him; he still gets to exist in some form. Yet, every time you feel the need to show off your intelligence and rationalise everything, you're ripping that hope away from him, and that's just fucking cruel.

I believe in this supernatural nonsense about as much as you do, but I also believe in hope, and I know the need for that is more important than the need to be right.'

Callum had tears forming in his eyes now. Grady fucking Daley. Of all his attempts over the years of insults and beatings had finally got him to cry.

Callum stood to his feet and extended his hand. It was now Grady's turn to get to his feet as he accepted the gesture.

'I think you're wrong about something though,' Callum spoke gently. 'I don't think it's going to take as much effort for you to be the person you want to be as you think. Ben sees it, I'm starting to see it, and I think before long, the people of this town will see it too.'

Grady embraced Callum with a prolonged hug.

CHAPTER EIGHT

Ben and Dale were returning to the mattresses, having spent some time exploring a few more of the rooms, not that Ben had been as enthused as before. Partly because it was much the same scene in every room as the others they had seen downstairs already, and partly because he was still down on Callum's rationalising of everything they had seen so far. Like a member of the audience watching a magic trick they know the secrets to, it lacked the same kind of marvel.

If there was any scant consolation to their time away from the other two, it would have appeared they had patched up their differences, and if nothing else, the stay here at Davenports would have been worth that alone.

Callum and Grady had been laughing hard at something when the others approached them. From what snippets of the conversation Ben had heard, they had been talking about a Monty Python Flying Circus episode which had been rerun on BBC2.

It was Callum who noticed Ben and Dale approaching them first. His laughter began to subside. Grady's silence was slower to catch up as it anticipated a potentially awkward conversation was about to take over.

'Hey, Ben,' Callum spoke with rare coyness. 'I just wanted to say, you know, I'm sorry. In my need to show how much I think, it turns out that sometimes I don't tend to think at all.'

'Don't sweat it,' Ben's amiable response came. 'I'm more relieved you two haven't killed each other in our absence.'

CHAPTER NINE

The four boys were laughing hard now, or in Ben's instance, as hard as his shortness of breath would permit.

The conversations, aided by the bottle of Southern Comfort, had regressed to an immature level, the way it should have been for boys their age trying hard not to think about the challenges which lay ahead. Boys will be boys, and tipsy boys will be juvenile.

Their current topic of conversation had started with who would win a fight between He-Man and the Incredible Hulk, but inevitably deteriorated to which character from the cartoon series, Masters of the Universe, they would most like a one-night stand with.

'Evil-Lyn for sure,' Grady spoke, not giving it a second thought.

'Are you nuts? The clue's in her name,' Ben responded. 'She's evil. You don't want to have a one-nighter with an evil person. If you don't call her back the next day, she's likely to stab you to death if she ever sees you again. It's like the eleventh commandment or something—bitches be crazy.'

'Yeah, but I bet she's dynamite in the sack,' Grady countered.

'What about her hairline, though? She's got hair like Bela Lugosi.' Ben adopted his mock-heavy European vampire accent again. 'I want to suck your dick.'

'At least she's got a fucking hairline, Termy,' Grady mocked, play-punching his friend gently in the arm.

'Touché,' his reply came. His verbal volley had been returned with an unplayable forehand.

'How about you, Private Reeves? A man of your moral compass would have to be Teela, right?'

Dale looked thoughtful before answering this question.

'Teela's a fine woman for sure,' he said. 'She's an auburn goddess and a good, strong, independent woman. I don't think I could do it to her though, the one-night stand, I mean. I genuinely think I'd cry whilst making love to her, knowing I'd be sneaking out on her while she's still sleeping. She doesn't deserve that. Plus, her dad's Man-at-Arms—he'd beat the living shit out of me if he ever found out what I did.'

'I wouldn't worry about Man-at-Arms,' Callum jumped in. 'I'd be too busy shagging him for him to care.'

The group laughed again.

'What about the Sorceress?' Grady asked with sincerity. 'She's smoking.'

'What?' the trio shouted back at him synchronised, almost as if it was choreographed.

'Why not?'

'She's fucking mental, that's why not,' Ben bit back, as if he was protecting his friend from making a real-life bad decision. 'She quite literally wears a dead bird on her head. Bitches be crazy, my friend, bitches be crazy.'

'Yeah,' Grady responded. 'But I bet she's...'

'Dynamite in the sack,' Ben and Dale finished his sentence for him.

'Just think, dude,' Dale added. 'She's a sorceress. Forget about Evil-Lyn—if you weren't to call her back, she'll turn you into a newt or something, or maybe even magic your dick into a marshmallow.'

Grady took another big gulp of the Southern Comfort before speaking again. His brain and mouth were becoming strangers in the night.

'Do you think Battle Cat ever takes massive cat shits during battle? And if so, do you think He-Man stops mid-fight to clean up after him? Also, speaking of shitting themselves, do you think Orko has a bum?'

The sound of Ben and Dale's laughing at Grady's random musings was abruptly cut short by a sudden gasp from Callum.

'Holy shit, I just saw something, guys,' he proclaimed, shaken. 'A shadow of a figure on the wall, a human figure.'

The boys began surveying the room, but other than the

rats, which appeared to be gradually growing in presence, there was nothing else in the hall.

'Nice try, Cal,' Ben spoke almost resentfully. 'But you don't have to pretend to see things on my behalf. You've already apologised, and that's enough.'

'I'm not pretending, I swear it.'

Ben stared deeply into Callum's eyes, trying to get the measure of him. There was a genuine glint of fear in them—he was telling the truth, or at least believed he was.

'It's probably just Joey fucking with us for shits and giggles on his long shift,' Ben reasoned, as deflated as a kid who'd found out the truth about Father Christmas for the first time.

'Then let's catch that shithead red-handed, shall we?' Grady spoke with glee as he made an instinctive grab for the walkie. He placed his finger to his mouth and then to his ear, signalling for the others to hush and keep an attentive listen. He then pressed the button to speak. Joey's voice came from the other end.

'Hey, what's up, little brother? Is everything OK?'

'Just checking in on you, bro, and wondering if you could settle an argument for me. I told the fellas that I could do the best impression out of the two of us of Brian Blessed from the Flash Gordon movie. I said it would be me, hands down.'

'You boys must be bored if that's what you're talking about, and high if you think it's true. Little brother, prepare to be shown up in front of your friends.'

The words 'Gordon's alive!' boomed down the radio very loud.

With the volume he bellowed the phrase, there was no way he could have been that loud and not been heard from within the building. Grady wasn't sure whether this was troubling him more, or the fact his brother was right in that he would have shown him up emphatically had this been a legitimate argument.

'You win,' Grady submitted as he ended the

conversation with Joey. 'Well, he sure as shit ain't inside here,' he clarified.

'I swear it, though, I saw the shadow of a person,' Callum repeated. 'Could there have been someone in here already? Maybe someone broke in on a different shift and Joey didn't notice? The door was locked when we got here and there are no signs of any broken windows, but that doesn't rule out someone being locked inside already. There's a lot of rooms inside this place, and it would be easy to stay one step ahead of Joey or the other security guards on their checks.'

'It can more likely be explained by the pot and drink in your system messing with your mind,' Ben spoke in his best impression of Callum, giving him a taste of his own medicine. 'It was just the power of suggestion beholden to the tales of this place making you see something that isn't. That's all.'

Callum digested these words—his own words—and smiled gently before nodding his head in agreement.

Ben may have been using his own thoughts and logic against him in a sarcastic, maybe even vengeful manner, but was that such a bad thing? They had been thoughts and logic he wholeheartedly believed in earlier that night, and nothing had changed since. Only his sobriety. A reality check in this place was what he needed right now, and he would take reality over the alternative of the stories about this place being true any day of the week.

Nonetheless, he gripped reassuringly onto one of the bottles of bourbon for comfort. Hell, the label even had that word on it. If they weren't alone, the glass vessel would make for an effective weapon if needed.

'Shall we go check it out to be on the safe side anyway?' Dale suggested. 'Just in case there is someone else in here?'

'Hell no,' Grady decried. 'Safe side be fucked. There's never anything safe about going to check things out. Have you ever seen a horror film before in your life? Unless it's The Burning, of course, which has probably got the greatest mass teen massacre scene of all time, then you never split up. And you never go hunting for trouble, as it will almost always end with a decapitation with a gardening or power tool.'

'I think Ben is right,' Callum submitted. 'It's more likely than not just a trick of the mind. It's nothing, don't start sweating over it.'

Although he'd dismissed the situation, and though he didn't want to raise the subject again, a sense of unease was coursing through Callum's body. He had always been so sure of his mind, but now there was doubt.

CHAPTER TEN

The song playing on the radio was 'She's Not There' by The Zombies.

The tune was abruptly cut short by the sound of static, interlaced with a backing track of disorientating and distorted audio, accompanied by ear-piercing feedback, which lasted for several seconds. Grady made an instinctive reach to change the station, but the broadcast resumed to normal by the time he could place a hand on the dial. Only this time, it wasn't 'She's Not There' playing, but 'We've Gotta Get Out of This Place' again. The song lasted for about a dozen seconds before the distorted sounds and feedback resumed, then switched back to the outro of 'She's Not There.'

'It sounds like the DJ is enjoying himself some Southern Comforts as well,' Grady quipped.

His attention turned to Dale, who appeared deep in concentration as he tried to distinguish the noises he had heard in the background of the feedback. It was almost as if they were the sounds of screeching tyres breaking hard on a road, accompanied by a male scream of sudden pain.

'So, Dale,' Grady continued.

Hearing his name brought his focus back into the room.

'I'm sure the other two have asked you this already, but why the hell did you sign up for the army, dude? I mean, that shit's hardcore, man. You're not a reprobate duffer like me, you're pretty switched on. Plus, you're still young. I'm sure there are loads of other career options out there for you to try before you fall back on marching and shooting for a living.'

'My mother asked me the same question when I told her I was going to enlist,' he replied amiably. 'She said I was too sweet-natured and a pacifist, and a pacifist in the army is about as welcome as a piranha in a bathtub.'

'Some pacifist you turned out to be, you kicked my arse

good and proper.'

'I did, but I did it for the right reasons. The answer to your question is the same I gave my mother.

My wanting to enlist came about when I was looking through a library book on the military one night to prepare for some homework assignment on World War 2 for history class. I came across a chapter on the Royal Engineers and what they do. Something that was mentioned was they build and repair bridges in war-torn areas, and I guess that really appealed to me. Maybe because I like the ideas of people being able to build bridges between each other as well as land. The principle is the same for both—you may have to dig deep to build those foundations before you begin, but before long, that connection is made and can withstand a hell of a lot of strain over the years.

Will my going to the army change the world? Of course not. Will it change people's attitudes? Probably not. Could it change complete strangers' lives for the better in a place where they need those bridges to be built, both between their land and their people? I'd like to think maybe it can, and that alone makes it worth it for me. My mother told me there's no place in the armed forces for a pacifist, yet I think it's the perfect place.'

Well, I hope it works out for you, bud,' said Grady. 'How about you, Cal? I know you're off to some fancy university and all, studying science, right? Whatcha hoping to do after that? Tempted to be a mad scientist and take over the world at all, like some Bond villain? With your brains, I reckon you could do it too. Just remember that we're cool now, right?'

There was no answer from Callum; he looked deep in thought over something, looking away from the others.

'Hey, Cal, what are you looking at, dude?' asked Dale.

There was no response.

Dale looked over to Ben and Grady and gave a perplexed shrug before turning his attention back towards Callum.

'Hello! Earth to Callum, come in Callum.'

Still no reply came.

Dale leaned over and placed his hand gently on Callum's shoulder. Despite the delicacy with which he touched him, Callum jolted hard at the sudden surprise.

'Jeez, Cal. Where's your mind at? You were away with the pixies just then.'

'The rats,' came his preoccupied reply.

'Fair enough, dude, whatever turns you on, I guess.'

Callum didn't rise to his friend's banter; instead, he pointed towards the direction of his gaze for the others to take a look too.

'I don't get what you're looking at, dude,' came Grady's response.

There were about a dozen rats approximately ten metres in front of them, maybe a higher number than he had seen as a group so far, but from what he could tell, there was nothing particularly interesting about them.

'Can't you see?' Callum sought to clarify. 'They're gathering.'

True enough, he was right. The dozen or so rats had formed into a group and were all facing the boys; more were approaching to join their number.

The boys watched, both amazed and intimidated as the vermin's numbers steadily increased. They were coming from the shadows and their nests, each of them joining the horde and facing the intruders to their domain. If this event wasn't unnerving enough, the fact these rodents weren't even displaying a solitary blink only served to alarm them further.

Within the space of a minute, there must have been over a hundred of them in their swarm.

'Er, guys,' Callum stated uneasily as he got to his feet. 'I'm starting to think that maybe there might be something to this place after all.'

'What the hell are they doing?' Grady asked as he joined Callum by his side.

'I don't know,' came Callum's reply. He hated not being

able to explain things. 'Maybe they're putting on a show of numbers to defend their terrain.'

'Or maybe they're just displaying their numbers to get ready to attack,' Dale spoke as he joined the other side of Callum. 'Look at their grouping, it's almost like that of a Roman legion.'

'Fucking great,' Grady cursed. 'Of all the rats we have to encounter, why the hell do they have to be the ones who have studied Roman Military tactics? What's Latin for, what the actual fuck?'

'Maybe it's time to get out of here,' said Callum.

'Yeah, I think you're right, fella,' Dale concurred.

Grady pulled the walkie-talkie from his pocket and pressed the button to speak to Joey. Only static could be heard.

The panic amongst the boys was palpable now. The breaths coming from them were understandably rapid and frightened.

'I've got a plan,' Grady spoke. 'I'll take out ten of the rats on the front row, you guys take out the other couple of hundred.'

'Not helping, dude,' Dale dismissed. 'Let's just leave all our shit and get out right now.'

'Agreed,' Callum panted.

Then it happened: the rats made their sudden move. Only to the boys' disorientating feelings of amazement, relief and disgust, it wasn't the humans they were making their attack on—it was each other. Those of the rats which weren't attacking another were nonchalantly mutilating themselves, gnawing at their legs and stomachs.

There was no squealing of pain coming from them, still no blinking.

'Ben, are you okay?' Dale asked, not taking his eyes from the mass mutilation. 'You've been a bit too quiet for my liking.'

There was no answer.

'Ben. Answer me, buddy.'

Callum turned his head to check on him while the other two kept their focus on the growing number of rats joining in this unnatural ritual. He wasn't there.

'Guys, he's gone.'

'What do you mean, he's gone?' Dale countered.

'As in, he's not here.'

It was Dale's turn to look behind. Just as Callum had stated, Ben had gone. He quickly surveyed the foyer and caught a glimpse of a figure halfway up the iron staircase.

'He's heading upstairs,' he informed the others.

'Shall we follow him?' Callum asked.

'We sure as shit ain't leaving him on his own,' Grady acknowledged. 'Besides, I'd rather be up there with him and away from these things.'

The trio of boys retreated to the staircase and began their ascent, Dale taking the lead and Grady bringing up the rear.

CHAPTER ELEVEN

Once upon the concourse of the top floor, Grady and Callum could see Dale's face was white as chalk, and his hand was trembling. He had turned to face the others, his mouth agape. He was trying to say something to the two boys, yet no words could escape him, just a meagre whimper.

Gripped tight between the forefinger and thumb of his quivering hand was one of Ben's Polaroids he had bent over to pick up from the floor.

If Dale's washed complexion alone wasn't enough to send further dread throughout them, it was the sight of tears running down his face that sealed the deal.

Callum patted him reassuringly on the shoulder and prised the photo from his trembling hand. He held it up so both he and Grady could see it. It was the Polaroid Grady had taken of Ben with Dale and Callum upon their first entering the manor. Yet there was a fourth figure present in the photograph.

Standing behind the boys, staring menacingly at the camera, was a person dressed in what appeared to be a Victorian-era dinner suit, and was a distinguished-looking male aged in his early forties. It was a figure they recognised in an instant from the local history books. Yet it couldn't be. It was Lord Davenport.

Callum let out a shriek of shock as the Polaroid burst into a sudden flame, causing him to drop it and instinctively extinguish it with his boot.

The trio all looked at each other; there were no words spoken, yet none were needed. Dale wasn't the only one with tears in his eyes now. The three of them had come to the sudden realisation that they were likely going to die in this place tonight.

'Ben!' Grady spoke with dejection. It was a voice that seemed to have already accepted defeat. 'We have to find him.'

'I don't think we need to look too hard,' Dale submitted as he pointed to a trail of other Polaroids on the floor.

It was like Hansel and Gretel leaving their trail of breadcrumbs, yet the boys doubted this trail was to help them find a way home—only entice them further into peril.

'You're not seriously considering following them?' Callum rued.

'What choice do we have?' Dale replied.

Callum thought of responding with a petulant comeback to show his disapproval, and he'd had some humdingers in mind, yet he chose to keep them to himself. Dale was right. They had no choice, not really—not unless they were to hightail it and leave their best friend in this place alone. Whatever malevolent forces were at play here, they had the boys over a barrel.

The trio tentatively followed the trail. Despite their better judgement, on occasion they would steal a glance at Ben's various discarded Polaroids, and each time they would see the same figure of Davenport in frame. He had been with them all this time.

Though neither of them dared say it aloud, they all had the same terrified thoughts gnawing away at them. Was he with them now, walking unseen behind?

The photograph trail ended, not that it mattered now. It was clear to the trio as to where Ben had gone.

A door was ajar, as if to simultaneously invite them and mock them. It was no surprise to the boys which room it had been.

Room 42.

CHAPTER TWELVE

Dale steadied his breath and gestured for the other two to hang back as he went on by himself towards the door of Room 42 to scout the room. He pulled the ajar door to him, as if to use it as a shield, before peering his head around it to look into the room.

'Ben,' he called out to no reply.

He yelled his name again, only this time louder. There was frustration in his voice now, as well as fear.

A few seconds later, Dale returned his attention to the other two. 'He's in there, but he's not responding.'

They both inched closer to join him and each took their turn to peer inside the room.

It was a disorienting room with no windows present. The walls had been painted green, with the floor and ceiling painted red and green in a zigzagged pattern. The only source of light came from a red bulb hanging from the ceiling with no lampshade around it. It hurt their eyes just to look into this room and made them feel an instant nausea, yet they imagined this had been the purpose of its interior decoration.

Unlike the other rooms they had seen thus far, there was no bedframe or mattress. It was empty. Empty, that was, save for the teenage boy standing in the corner of the room with his back to the entrance.

'Ben!' Dale called out. Again, there was no acknowledgement, no indication he had heard his friend's words. He knew he would have to go in to physically retrieve him.

'You two stay here,' he ordered.

'Fuck you,' Grady defied. 'We all stay together, no matter what. I'm not letting you do something stupid all by yourself. Making dumb decisions is my specialist subject. I'm going in with you. What was it those Muskerhounds said in that Dogtanian cartoon they turned into an old book?

One for all and all for one?'

Despite the direness of the situation, Callum couldn't help but smile. He was unsure whether Grady fucking Daley was joking around with that ridiculous statement or truly was that oblivious to classic literature. Either way, he appreciated his words as it broke some of his tension, if only a little.

'Yeah, there's no way I'm staying out here all by myself,' Callum contributed. 'Let's go rescue our D'Artagnan.'

Dale nodded his appreciation.

The three of them entered the room and made their beeline to the corner of the room and for Ben.

The loudness of the door slamming shut behind them seemed excessive, causing each of them to jolt—even Ben, who was suddenly awakened from his trance.

'This used to be Davenport's favourite room,' Ben spoke weakly. 'Not all of us are going to be getting out of it alive.'

CHAPTER THIRTEEN

'Ben, are you okay?' Dale asked as he rushed over to check on his friend.

Ben nodded his head, though not with any conviction. For the first time since they had been here, Dale could see terror in his eyes.

'It's locked,' Grady called out to them.

There was no handle or knob on the inside of the door. Nothing for them to grip onto to pull it open.

Callum gestured for him to get out of the way so he could try. He was met with the same failed result.

'Yeah, it's locked.'

'No shit,' Grady snapped. 'I just fucking said that, didn't I?' Any goodwill they had been feeling towards each other earlier was being washed away with a surge.

Dale gestured for the two of them to simmer down. Raising voices and getting heated wasn't going to help anyone right now – if anything at all could help them now. In order to divert Callum and Grady's attention from each other, he directed them towards Ben.

'What did you mean, dude? You said not all of us are going to leave this room alive.'

'He won't let us,' Ben's answer came. 'Davenport, I mean.'

'How do you know this?' Callum intervened.

'He told me.'

'How?'

'When you've been knocking on death's door for as long as I have, eventually, you're going to be let in for a chat,' Ben elaborated. 'He showed me things that have happened in this room, such terrible things. He says that he welcomes us into his home, but if you are to stay, then you must abide by his rules.'

'Well, I hope that arsehole's rules are something as basic as we have to take our shoes off,' Grady quipped.

The solemn look upon Ben's face suggested this wasn't the case.

'The only way he'll open the door for us to get out of this room is for one of us to be sacrificed to him. It's always been the way any of his "guests" have ever left this room.' Ben began to run his hands down the wall closest to him.

'This room has always been the most special to him out of all the rooms in this house - his blood is literally a part of it. When constructing the manor, his blood was shed following one of his rituals and mixed into the mortar which helped bind these walls together.

Very little was known about Davenport before his arrival in Hulmsford. Yet, his prior alias, Barnabus Scott, had been gaining increasing amounts of unwanted attention in the north of England for his satanic beliefs and gatherings of depravity.

Barnabus Scott fled in the middle of the night with his riches and his flock of followers before his inevitable arrest and trial could muster. He arrived in Hulmsford posing as Lord Archibald Davenport with his followers under the guise of his staff.

The outbreak of Tuberculosis within the town soon after the completion of his manor's construction was no coincidence. It had been fabricated at his behest. All it took was the bribery of a local doctor with the promise of a substantial share of Davenport's inflated wealth for him to misdiagnose one of the townsfolk suffering from simple influenza as Tuberculosis.

As hysteria and fear over this disease spread through the town, it became easy for this corrupt doctor to misdiagnose an increasing number of people without challenge or suspicion.

With Davenport offering his manor up as a sanitarium and currying favour amongst the people of Hulmsford as a consequence, he soon found himself revered by the locals. Little did they know the despicable truth.

As signs of illness in the town began to subside,

however, no more so than in the warmer weather, Davenport's followers resorted to abductions to ensure the manor was well enough populated for their master's insidious intentions.

The patients, sent here under false pretence, or seized in the night, were systematically and mercilessly tortured and experimented upon as Davenport sought to perfect his practice of black magic and worship of dark deities. Often, the victims here were pitted against each other in locked rooms, forced to fight for food, water, and the prolonging of their futile survival.

Of all these rooms, Room 42 – this room – was the most feared. The only thing able to escape it without Davenport's permission were the screams.

Even a hundred years after his execution, with his malignant blood encased in its foundations, he was still a part of this house, and this house was very much a part of him.

In 1917, when the government came into this place to use it as a military psychiatric hospital, Davenport didn't appreciate their noble intentions. Nor did he appreciate it when they decided to redecorate it - especially his cherished Room 42.

They had painted the room from the green and reds you see before you now into a sterile, calming white, but Davenport has changed it back to its former glory tonight, just for us.

This was the room used as the main counselling room by the therapist brought in to help rehabilitate those poor officers suffering from shellshock. This was the room where the first of the Hope and Glory killings occurred.

What that therapist, Dr Katherine Harkness, didn't realise whilst she was conducting these therapy sessions was that she wasn't the only one talking to those poor souls.

Whilst she was counselling them in the hope of lifting them from their trauma, Davenport was whispering malevolently into their ears, telling them all the devilish details of this place's heinous past and that any hope they had of leaving this place was futile. They would be better served by killing themselves here – and each other.

It was on 19th January, during one of the daily therapy sessions with Dr Harkness, that Captain Sidney Pendergrove was unable to resist Davenport's serpentine suggestions any further.

Pendergrove had already been seen as one of the more troubled residents of Hope and Glory and had recently been displaying signs of self-harm, the latest injury being that he had used the wall of his bedroom to prise the nails away from his fingers by clawing repeatedly at it. He had also been spreading disruption and panic throughout his fellow patients with talk of Lord Davenport and his dark beliefs and worship.

It was when Harkness had probed Pendergrove during a conversation over the fresh wounds on his fingers that she asked more about Lord Davenport.

'What does he say to you?' she had asked.

'That I must kill you,' Pendergrove's nonchalant reply came.

'And why is that?' she asked further.

'For his amusement.'

'There is nothing amusing about death,' she responded as she made some notes on her pad.

'That's a nice pen,' Pendergrove observed, changing the subject. 'Is it a Parker?'

Harkness instinctively looked down at the silver biro despite already knowing it was.

'It is,' she confirmed. 'I appear to have misplaced my Waterman fountain pen yesterday.'

'That's a shame,' Pendergrove commented, at last showing traces of interest. 'That was a nice quality pen.'

'It was,' Harkness agreed, making a mental note of this sudden shift in demeanour and topic. 'I didn't realise you had such an interest in pens.'

'Well, you know what they say, ma'am. The pen is

mightier than the sword.'

With these words barely finished, Pendergrove had made a sudden and forceful lunge towards Harkness, toppling her and her chair backwards. Pendergrove allowed a few moments for her to release a scream of help, then he reached into his pocket to reveal her lost fountain pen.

'Such a fine quality pen,' he stated again before driving it into her face and throat repeatedly, and with increasing force. The pointed nib piercing her flesh with each strike.

A trio of orderlies stormed into the room to restrain Pendergrove and to give Harkness the medical attention her bloodied and mutilated face and throat was in desperate need of.

The orderlies had been standing on alert outside Room 42 when they heard the screams. Patient violence had always been a risk given the trauma of the trenches the residents here had experienced, yet upon Harkness's insistence, the need for one-on-one private interactions was far more of a priority than her safety. As such, a compromise had been reached that the orderlies would be on standby outside Room 42 when the sessions were being conducted, just in case they were needed.

No sooner than they had entered the room and made their way to Harkness and Pendergrove, the door had slammed shut behind them - seemingly of its own accord.

Pendergrove ceased all signs of a struggle as two of the orderlies restrained him, instead displaying a satisfied smile as he watched the third orderly attempt in vain to slow the bleeding coming from the punctured jugular of Harkness. It was too late though; she was already dead.

With the patient's struggles stopped and his colleagues in control of him, the third orderly made his way to the door so he could summon more aid and medical supplies.

As he went to turn the doorknob, he emitted a sudden cry of pain, a yelp that was accompanied in synchronicity by the odour of burning flesh. As the orderly attempted to withdraw his hand from the metal doorknob, strings of melted flesh from his palm came with it.

'The knob, it's like lava,' the orderly yelled in pain as he examined his wounds.

'He won't let you leave,' Pendergrove laughed.

One of the orderlies who had hold of Pendergrove shifted his grip around him at hearing these laughs. He was no longer restraining the patient; he was strangling him. Even as he was being choked to his death, Pendergrove's smile refused to falter. The orderly's hands then found themselves around the throat of his colleague beside him.

Outside Room 42, Hope and Glory's administrator, Captain Harold Moss, was frantic with his rattling of the door handle.

'What's going on in there?' he shouted through the locked door. 'Dr Harkness? Staff? We heard screams.'

Moss turned his attention to one of the orderlies on the ground floor.

'You, sir, get me an axe. We're going to have to break the door down.'

The orderly nodded his head and ran off to get the tool as ordered. Moss continued his futile rattling of the door handle and shouting.

'Can somebody answer me, please? What is going on in there? Is everybody safe?'

Moss could sense a figure standing next to him now, observing him.

'That was quick,' Moss spoke, assuming it was the orderly.

There was no answer.

Moss turned to face him.

Instead of seeing the orderly, it was one of the patients; he had a vacant look upon his face.

'You need to be back in your room, sir,' Moss stated with calm assertion.

'There is no hope,' the patient stated as he held his hands in the air to show Moss—they were covered in blood and excrement. Before Moss could say anything, the patient had grabbed him by the back of the head and had begun driving it repeatedly into the outside wall of Room 42, crying uncontrollably as he did so, yet unable to stop his violent actions. Unable to stop the voice inside his head urging him to continue for his amusement.

A riot had begun throughout Hope and Glory; the patients had all made their way from their rooms. There was death in the air, just as Davenport had whispered to them there would be, and they would be his tools to ensure there would be more.

Those patients who had not turned on the staff felt obliged to turn on each other, and if they could not turn on anyone else in their immediate vicinity, they turned on themselves. Some electing to jump from the balcony of the conclave with grateful smiles upon their faces.

By the time the orderly who had been tasked with retrieving the axe at the orders of his supervisor returned to the site of bloody carnage, he did so to the aftermath of the sick, the dead and the dying. Peers and patients alike.

He clasped the axe tight, praying he wouldn't have to use it in self-defence, but knowing that, if it came down to it, he wouldn't hesitate to use it.

Confused and frightened over how so much destruction could have occurred in the five minutes it had taken him to exit through the rear of Hope and Glory and to the storage shed where the maintenance tools were kept under lock and key and return, the grand hall had turned into the aftermath of a warzone. Yet, he had heard no screams, no yells of aggression coming from inside here.

The orderly surveyed the scene for any fellow staff members. His gaze fell on a couple of the nurses cowering in the corner, hiding behind the mutilated corpses of a couple of patients which they had used to shield them from the dangers.

The orderly looked at the axe in his hand and realised how much of a threat he must have looked to them too. He submissively placed it on the floor.

'It's okay,' he assured. 'I'm not going to hurt you. What the hell has happened here?'

'Hell is exactly what happened here,' one of the nurses sobbed as she cautiously approached him.

'We need to call the authorities,' he spoke.

'And tell them what?' the nurse replied, still whimpering. 'Look around you. It won't make any difference what we tell them. They won't believe us.'

Just then, the sound of a door creaking open could be heard from the first floor. It was Room 42.

An orderly exited the room, his white uniform covered in smears of blood. He was smiling.

'Oh my God,' the nurse gasped as she saw he had removed his own eyeballs and was holding them proudly on display in his cupped palms.

'Davenport sends his regards,' the orderly spoke as he walked blindly towards the railings of the concourse.

Upon reaching and making a feel for it, he casually climbed over and performed a belly flop to the ground below.

The government cleaned up the scene of the incident as they tried to make sense of what happened, and the surviving witnesses were sworn to secrecy over their statements. You know what secrets are like, however; very seldom do they remain that way. The truth always finds a way of getting out, or at least versions of the truth.

The others could tell from the haunted look upon Ben's face that what he had been telling them about Hope and Glory had been the truth, or at least what had been relayed to him by Davenport.

As if he didn't have enough shit to deal with already, he now had the knowledge of what had really happened here to deal with too. He'd been given the answers he had been looking for about this place, and now he had, oh how he wished he could go back to the innocence of wondering again.

'Hey, what happened to those poor souls won't happen

to us,' Callum defied. 'Those patients here were already suffering from mental illness and were more susceptible to Davenport's whispers. They had already seen far more violence and bloodshed through their experiences in the war than any person should, and Davenport used that to his advantage to manipulate them. That bastard is trying to prime us to turn on each other too, can't you see?

That bloody ritual by the rats, him showing Ben the events of what happened knowing that he'd relay it to us all. All this visceral violence is being done to get us worked up. We're stronger than that, all of us. We've just got to stay that way.'

'It won't be as easy as that,' Ben replied.

'Yeah, well since when have any of us had it all our own way in our lives? Why should now be any different?' Grady replied. 'Hey, Dale. Do you reckon we could break that door down between us? It's solid, right, but you're pretty solid too, and not to blow my own dick, I'm not exactly a wet paper bag. What say we alternate it? Focussed bursts.'

'It's worth a shot, I guess.'

The two of them made their way to the back of the room.

'Age before beauty,' Dale gestured.

'Shit before the shovel?' Grady returned with a sly smile.

Dale took a deep breath and sprinted towards the solid oak door, turning in at the last moment before impact. He bounced off it and gave his shoulder a little rub.

'Could take a while,' he panted.

'It won't work,' Ben uttered weakly to himself.

Grady elected to ignore him. It was his turn now. He put in the same amount of effort and was met with the same result.

'Shall we make it interesting?' he challenged Dale. 'A fiver for whoever breaks it down.'

'Yeah sure, why not?' Dale accepted as he took another run at it.

For the next five minutes, the two of them took turns in

tandem to take runs at the door. With each failed attempt, their energy and spirits were being sapped. They were already blowing heavy and displaying signs of defeat upon their infuriated faces.

'Give it up guys,' Ben pleaded, 'it's no good.'

'What other fucking options do we have?' Grady bit back with venom.

He was aware he was falling back into his old traits of letting anger and frustration dictate his mouth, and he was lashing out at the only person he truly considered a friend—but this was still the same person who had talked him into coming to this place, knowing full well of its reputation. This was all his fault, and he was resenting him for it.

'Let's simmer down,' Dale tried to intervene with a delicate blend of calm and assertiveness.

'Remember what Cal said, he wants us to turn on each other. He's priming us to lose control of our emotions and let him in.

It's just like my old P.E. teacher used to do to us before a rugby match. He'd get us so worked up, that come kick-off, we went into berserker mode as soon as the whistle blew. We ended up losing far more games than we won, of course. A cunning fox will always win out over a headless chicken.

The crazy thing is, I don't think my teacher even cared if we won or lost, he just wanted to watch the carnage, simply because he could. I wouldn't mind betting this Davenport arsehole is the same.'

'So, what are you saying we do then, nothing?' asked Grady.

'I can't think of anything that will throw him off his game plan more.'

'That's right,' Callum spoke. 'So, we wait it out in here for a few hours. Joey's outside, right? Come dawn, he'll come in and check on us and let us out then, one way or another.'

Ben emitted a heavy sigh of frustration. 'Do you really

think it will be that easy?' he asked. Yet the others paid him no notice. He was back to being the invisible kid again.

'Might not even have to wait that long,' Grady replied as he smugly pulled out the walkie-talkie from his pocket.

Grady's swagger of cockiness was soon contorted into a disturbed demeanour as he pressed the button to talk to Joey.

Instead of hearing his brother's voice, a plethora of anguished screams came through the airwaves. Tortured voices begging for mercy and a swift death, yelling for help from unseen forces from either above or below to end their suffering.

Grady fumbled frantically to switch off the walkie, not that he feared it would make any difference—the voices of the tortured souls he had heard would stay with him for the rest of his life, however long or short that would turn out to be.

The others saw the distraught expression on Grady's face. Though it was obvious he hadn't got through to his brother, they each chose not to push him on what he had heard—his troubled look was enough to tell them they were best off not knowing.

A silence befell the room for several minutes, each of the boys elected to keep their thoughts to themselves, not wanting to spread further despair or paranoia.

The quiet was broken by Callum.

'Can you feel that?' he asked. 'Is it me, or is this room getting hotter?'

'I told you he wouldn't make it that easy for you,' Ben tried to reason.

The others could feel it now. The temperature within the room was being cranked up somehow, and not to a pleasant level. This was real heat, suffocating heat. If the four boys were intent on playing with fire by coming to this place, it was only right that they feel its burn. The room was becoming a furnace, and its cinders were starting to sear.

'I told you already,' Ben spoke. 'There's only one way

Davenport is going to let most of us out of here, and that's for one of us not to. Listen guys, I'm a dead man walking anyway. It may as well be me who doesn't make it out. It will be a mercy killing in a way.'

'You can quit talking that kind of crap right now, you wazzock,' Dale shot down. 'No one here is killing you. No one here is killing anybody.'

'Many others before us had similar intentions of defiance too,' Ben countered. 'Maybe we'll hold out for an hour or so, but we'll succumb eventually.'

'He's right,' Callum spoke. 'We'll be dehydrated, disorientated, and desperate before long.'

'There's got to be a way out,' Dale defied with stubbornness as he scrutinised the door. 'Sometimes it's the most obvious answers which are hardest to see.'

'Yeah, well whilst you're examining the door, dude, I'll be sitting here in the corner saving my strength,' said Grady. 'Just in case you do break and come for me,' he continued in his mind.

******

What felt like an age had passed. It was hard for the boys to gauge how much time they had spent in Room 42 since their watches had all stopped working once inside there.

'Do you think it's just our watches that have stopped, or time itself?' Dale pondered.

Usually, Callum had an explanation for everything, yet with logic and science meaning nothing to him inside this house, this room, he had never felt so lost, so clueless, so dumb. Instead, he sat silently in the corner of the room opposite Grady.

The thoughts of if he would be able to kill him, if it truly came down to it, were never far from the forefront of Callum's mind. Sure, there had been no love lost between Grady and himself, yet there was a colossal difference between love lost and life lost.

As he searched his soul for an answer, he doubted Grady's soul needed to be delved so deep into.

Though he believed Grady was sincere in trying to be a better person, and that he truly felt repentant over his treatment of him and others, the fact of the matter was the bullying side of him would always be inside of him deep down, waiting for something to stir and agitate it back to the surface—and the current predicament they found themselves in was surely such an event.

Then there was Dale. He trusted him, of course he did. Yet, he had enlisted in the army, had he not? And are they not expected to kill in situations far less dire than what they found themselves in now? Yeah, Dale claimed to be a pacifist, but when life and death are on the line and primal urges take over any sense of moral aptitude, such noble claims can be thrown out of the window. Well... if this room had a window.

Paranoia aside, it was the heat, dehydration, distress and disorientation playing havoc with Callum's mind the most. Yet as another indecipherable volume of time passed, he could smell something in this room now as well. Just as the heat had done, the aroma was gradually growing stronger. It was the stench of excrement.

'What's that smell?' he asked.

'I can't smell anything,' Dale replied.

'How can you not? It smells so strong,' said Callum. 'It smells like shit.'

'I may have let out a sneaky fart or two, sorry,' said Grady. His voice sounded exhausted and beaten. 'I tried to hold it in, I thought I'd got away with it too.'

'No, it's not that,' said Callum. 'Are you sure you can't smell it? It's so strong.'

The others shook their heads.

Callum was trying his hardest not to gag at the odour now. Even if the others couldn't smell the putrid stench invading his sinuses with all the subtlety of a stink bomb in a cake shop, if he were to vomit, they would most definitely be able to smell that—and with this heat and stuffiness, it would be sure to set off a chain reaction. A pukelear bomb.

'You did this.'

Callum heard a slurred but familiar voice in an accusing tone. It was Mr Hutchins, his old chemistry teacher. The aroma of shit was somehow even stronger now, mixed in with traces of cheap coffee and cheaper whisky.

Callum could see his former teacher standing in the centre of the room. He was wearing his ever-present grey suit and patterned blue and red tie and was carrying an almost empty bottle of spirits. His eyes were red raw. Callum was unsure whether it was from tears or alcohol. Likely, it was both.

One thing he was certain of, however, was that these eyes were staring at him with the same intensity as the last time he had seen him outside the school. He could see now, it was a stare of accusation and hatred, a stare that lusted for vengeance. 'You did this,' the figure repeated.

Callum looked around the room to see if any of the others could see the apparition. Their lack of any reaction other than curiosity and concern over the evident fear on his face was enough of an indication it was only he who could see him.

'You okay, mucka?' Dale asked him.

Callum unpersuasively nodded his head. He tried convincing himself it was just the delirium causing this hallucination, much like a desert mirage. Even now, after all that was happening in this room, he was trying to logicise events. Yet a hallucination wouldn't account for the overwhelming smell.

'You did this,' the figure spoke again. He inched slowly closer to Callum each time he spoke this sentence.

'I'm sorry,' Callum whimpered. 'It was only meant as a joke.'

'You did this.'

Another step closer.

'Hey dude, what's going on?' Grady asked with genuine concern. Yet Callum failed to acknowledge him. His frightened eyes were focused on something else.

Callum could see the bottle in Hutchins' hand was different now—it was broken.

Another step closer.

'You did this.'

Hutchins raised the broken vessel towards his throat. The jagged shards were caressing his jugular.

Callum knew the figure in the room wasn't really there with him, yet he couldn't help but call out to him.

'Wait, stop!' he pleaded.

'You did this.'

Hutchins was just a step in front of Callum now. The tears of the boy were falling fast.

Hutchins began to rake the broken shards across his throat before dropping to the ground.

'Cal!' Dale spoke as he shook him out of his apparent daze. He could see a patch on his jeans darken and some yellow liquid escape onto the floor where he was sitting. 'Speak to me, fella.'

Cal looked around the room, still petrified. Hutchins was gone now, as had the smell. It was just the three boys with him. Each was staring with concern.

'It was Hutchins, he was here,' Callum sobbed. 'I mean, his ghost was here. He committed suicide. He'd killed himself because of that prank I pulled. It was only meant as a joke to bring him down a peg or two over how he was treating his pupils. I never in a million years intended for him to sink so low that he'd kill himself over what happened.'

'You don't know that he did,' said Dale. 'It could be this place just playing a trick on you, to mess up your mind. To get you weak and desperate, so Davenport can get his claws into you.'

'We've got to get out of here,' Cal continued to sob. 'I've wet myself.'

As he said this last part, his eyes fell on Grady. He didn't know why he should declare his accident to his former bully. Maybe he felt he needed to be made to feel like shit over what he had done to Hutchins.

'Hey, don't sweat it,' Grady spoke with empathy. 'I've got a spare pair of shell-suit bottoms in my rucksack. You can change into them once we find a way to get back downstairs and out of this dump.'

Callum burst into harder tears now. How pathetic must he have looked? he thought. Even Grady fucking Daley was being considerate of him now.

'We've just got to ride this out,' Grady continued. Though his words were intended to be encouraging, they were betrayed by the exhaustion in his voice. 'I don't think it's got any hotter in here than it was about ten minutes ago. Hell, I've had worse burning sensations on my skin from my Insignia deodorant spray. All we have to do is be calm and not do anything stupid. Joey will come and get us, he has to, right?'

The others didn't know if he was right or not, but they had to believe in him. They had to believe in his defiance, his pig-headedness. If there was an occasion when they needed him to be a stubborn, petulant prick, then it was now.

The four of them sat in silence for a while longer, heads down and not wanting to look at each other. Partly because they didn't want anyone else to see the struggles on their faces, but partly because they didn't want to witness any more ghosts from their past.

A sudden scream from Dale broke the silence. It was a penetrating yell of both fear and pain. His breaths were rapid now, and his usually stoic face displayed rare signs of duress and panic. He calmed himself as he took reassurance from the faces of his friends, no matter how concerned they looked.

'Dude!' Ben spoke with concern.

'I'm okay,' Dale unconvincingly assured. 'It's just I felt

something. It didn't last long, but it was an intense heat, much hotter than this room, and it felt as though my body was being torn apart. It was almost as if I was experiencing an explosion. It felt so real.' A few moments after making his statement, his anguished scream of pain came again. And it would continue to do so intermittently over what felt like half an hour.

'We've got to make it stop,' Callum stated.

'I know how,' a weak voice came. It was Ben.

'What? How?' Grady replied with sudden optimism. It was to be a sanguinity short-lived.

'I love you guys,' Ben spoke. 'I want to thank you for being my friends, and I'm sorry I put you in this situation.'

Before the others could fully comprehend what Ben was saying or intending, he had already stood up and placed both hands in his jeans pockets. He extended his tongue as much as he could and clasped his teeth around it.

Once the others had realised his plan, it was already too late. They would never have had time enough to get up to their feet and restrain him.

Ben performed a standing jump about a foot in the air. It wasn't the height of his jump that was important; it was the force with which he landed on the hard tile floor. His landing wasn't so much a dive but a belly flop as he impacted the floor jaw-first.

The force of the landing was not enough to sever the tongue completely. It was still attached by a thread—yet the damage had been done. The blood was gushing out of it and down his throat, slowly choking him. A secondary wound had also been inflicted on his chin from the impact and was pumping out blood—he would surely be in need of stitches for the gash.

'What do we do?' Grady panicked.

'First things first, we've got to get him in the recovery position so he's not choking on his blood,' Dale spoke.

He had read some first-aid books in preparation for his army training and knew he had to make sure the airways were as unrestricted as possible. This was easier said than done though; Ben was purposely fighting against his efforts to place him in the recovery position.

'Goddammit!' Dale cried with rare panic and frustration as he attempted to hold Ben into place. He was already beginning to choke. 'I'm sorry, mucka,' he spoke as he launched a hefty left hook into his friend's jaw, knocking him unconscious as a consequence. His accuracy with his clubbing blow had been impressive. His clenched fist avoided the open wound under his chin.

He placed Ben into recovery and opened his mouth to release some of the oozing blood building up inside of it.

Dale curled his fingers into a hook shape and placed them inside Ben's mouth.

He couldn't help but cringe as he felt the lacerated tongue—it was still attached, but barely. He didn't know how much longer it would manage to stay that way since it wouldn't take much pressure to finish the job, even with Ben out cold.

As such, Dale knew he would have to keep his hands on his head and jaw to keep his mouth open.

Callum pulled off his t-shirt and rolled it up to press against the chasm of a cut on the chin. It wouldn't be enough to stop the gushing flow of bleeding, but maybe it would slow it down at least.

The t-shirt may have been sodden with his sweat from the room's heat, and any risk of infection into the wound could prove a fatal one, but beggars could not be choosers right now.

'Fuck!' Grady shouted with frustration.

He looked at the state Ben was in and knew that should they make it out of here alive, he would remain a mess. Even if the surgeons felt they could salvage his tongue, that would likely mean an operation, and would the doctors even want to risk it with him?

Throughout Grady's friendship with Ben, he had never tried to display pity for him, yet as he looked at him lying there unconscious, bleeding heavily and self-mutilated, how could he display anything but pity for him? He eyed the door again; he needed to take out his anger on something. It was clear he was going to make another charge at it.

'Jesus, Grade,' Callum sighed. 'You've tried that already. Save your energy.'

'For what, exactly? A slow death?' he snapped. 'Fuck that and fuck you. I'd rather die from trying something than die from doing nothing.'

He made his latest run for the door. It was clear his charge lacked the same zip and energy as previously. The impact was little more than a polite connection rather than any destructive collision. He trudged to the opposing side of the room, ready to try again.

He took a few more moments to compose himself and reclaim some much-needed breath, then he made his next attempt. He wasn't so much of a raging bull, but a slightly perturbed calf. Nonetheless, he'd put everything he had left into his run. Then it happened: the door swung open of its own accord, milliseconds before Grady was about to make impact with it.

Grady attempted to slow himself, yet the momentum, coupled with the short distance of the concourse from the room to the balcony, meant he was unable to stop before he reached the metre-high railing. He had enough presence of mind to reach out for it and make a grab, yet it wasn't enough to prevent him toppling over.

CHAPTER FOURTEEN

Grady's instinctive grab onto the railing was tight enough to prevent him falling to the hard floor beneath—at least for now. He had managed to desperately reach up and clasp the rail with his free hand, but despite both hands gripped tight, he wasn't sure how long he would be able to hold on.

Even had his strength not been so sapped from the ordeal of Room 42, it would have been a struggle to pull himself up, but now, with him at his weakest, it was surely only a matter of time—likely seconds before he would have to concede defeat.

The drop was around eight metres, maybe not enough to kill him if he landed favourably, but with the hard marble floor waiting in welcome, even landing properly in this instance would result in some broken bones.

He could feel his sweaty grip loosen, and the burn of his muscles mocked him. He began to brace himself for the inevitable fall.

Upon conceding defeat and letting go, however, instead of falling, he felt something grab onto both his wrists.

Grady let out a desperate sigh of relief at his reprieve.

'Dale?' he spoke.

There was no answer.

Grady looked upwards yet could see there was no one above him. He felt pain in his wrists now, as if someone was purposely digging their fingernails into them, breaking through the skin. He let out a grimace, then he felt the grip release him.

Grady plummeted.

CHAPTER FIFTEEN

Even though Callum, Dale and the still-unconscious Ben escaped Room 42 as soon as the door flung open, it was already too late for Callum to reach Grady in time.

The sound of a hard impact, accompanied by the sickening crunch of breaking bones, was loud and penetrating enough to have travelled up to the first floor.

If there was any scant reassurance to be found from Grady's subsequent screams of excruciating pain, it meant that he was still alive—but at what cost?

Callum rushed over to the guard rail and peered below. The unnatural angle of Grady's right foot indicated it had twisted more than a Chubby Checker record.

As disturbing as the sight was of the sole of his right foot being skewed in excess of 90 degrees, it was nothing compared to the state of Grady's left leg. Even from Callum's elevated position, he could see the flow of red saturating Grady's trousers.

The cause of this wound was clear from the unnatural bulge in the shin area pushing up against the fabric of the jeans—the shin bone had snapped upon landing and pierced through the skin.

'Hang on in there, Grade,' Callum yelled down. 'We'll come and grab you, then we're getting the fuck out of dodge.'

'I wouldn't count on that,' Callum could decipher through Grady's anguished groans of pain.

It was only when Callum began to make his way down the spiral staircase that he realised what Grady had meant.

'How the hell?' Dale wheezed from behind him.

He was making his way down more tentatively due to having Ben upon his shoulder in a fireman's lift. It was all he could do to stop his legs from buckling under him, though this had nothing to do with the deadweight he was carrying—it was to do with the sudden sense of despair upon laying eyes on the front entrance to Davenport Manor.

A multitude of bedframes from the manor's rooms had been used to form a barricade against the door and windows. The frames were twisted and intertwined with each other. There was no way of simply walking out now.

CHAPTER SIXTEEN

Callum rushed over to Grady whilst Dale delicately placed Ben onto one of the mattresses they had been using as their base. His bleeding appeared to have slowed down a little, yet he was still losing more than he could afford.

Dale placed him back into the recovery position to be extra cautious. Callum's t-shirt, which had been used as a makeshift bandage for the gash on the chin, had become sodden with blood. Dale reached into his backpack and pulled out his spare t-shirt and rolled it up to press against the wound. He couldn't help but take note of how much colour had been drained from Ben's face, even by his trademark pale standard.

The radio was still playing. It was some '70s disco track Dale didn't recognise. Though disco music had never been his bag, he paid the radio some extra attention, if only to deduce from the genre playing what the time would have been. By his reckoning, the time would have been between three and four in the morning.

Disco Dave's Night Owl Hour must have been the programme. Not a show he enjoyed even at the best of times, and this was most certainly far from that.

He pulled a bottle of water from his backpack and took a grateful and hefty gulp as he stood vigil over Ben.

******

'I'm pretty fucked, ain't I?' Grady spoke as Callum approached. 'I don't need to be as smart as you are to figure that much out.'

Grady was sitting upright and couldn't help but morbidly stare at his heinous injuries. His jean leg was rolled up to reveal the shin bone peering out of his flesh like a prairie dog poking its head up from the sand.

He had seen no end of elaborate blood and guts special

effects from the horror videos he had watched far too many of in his time, and he had to concede the state his legs were in wouldn't have looked out of place even in one of the more visceral of the Italian Giallos.

'You're no more fucked than the rest of us,' the dry response came. 'I'm going to have to carry you over to the mattresses,' Callum explained. 'Are there any snide comments about this incredible queer having to manhandle you that you want to get out of the way first?'

'I think we're way past that point now, buddy,' Grady replied, trying to force a smile through the grimace.

'I'll try to be as delicate as I can, okay, Grade?'

'It's going to hurt like a sonofabitch no matter what, so just do what you got to do. Call it karma for all the times I beat you up.'

Callum nodded as he tried to manoeuvre into position to scoop Grady up to carry him. Though he tried putting on as reassuring a face as he could muster, he couldn't disguise the disgust as he got in closer to Grady's limbs.

'I don't think I'll be getting picked for the football team next Saturday,' Grady attempted to laugh off for Callum's benefit.

'The sad fact is you'd still get picked ahead of me,' Callum quipped back. 'Ready on three. One, two, three.'

Grady let out a yelp of pain as Callum shovelled him up from under his legs as if he was Richard Gere carrying Debra Winger in 'An Officer and a Gentleman.' Cal even began to sing its theme song, 'Up Where We Belong,' but as Grady let out a laugh at this, he immediately produced another yell of pain.

'Sorry,' said Callum.

'Don't sweat it.'

Callum made his way over to the mattresses to join Dale and the unconscious Ben and lowered Grady gently down next to him. The mattresses were fast beginning to resemble a field hospital. He looked over to Dale, whose spirits looked as broken as Grady's limbs.

The Last Night – Steve McElhenny

No words were spoken between the two of them, yet no words were needed. They both knew the direness of the situation.

Dale took a new unopened bottle of water from his backpack and offered it to Grady—it was something he was only too grateful for.

Callum pulled out his spare t-shirt from his rucksack and put it on as Dale and he began surveying the landscape, which had changed so much since they'd left this spot for their upstairs ordeal.

To their south was the sea of mutilated rats. The stench of their wounds, already turning rotten, assaulted the boys' sinuses with as much welcome as a fart in a church.

To their north was the barricade of the twisted, intertwined bedframes. East and West were the perimeter of rooms, all the doors were wide open to them as if to invite them in.

'What's your thoughts?' Dale asked.

'Nothing positive,' Callum replied. 'We can't go out the front way with that barricade blocking the doors and windows. With four of us fit, maybe, just maybe, we'd have been able to drag it enough to squeeze through, but just the two of us, we'd have no chance of shifting it.

'There's bound to be a rear doorway to this place, but trying to find it is not a gamble I'm willing to take right now. Even if we didn't have Ben and Grady to carry, what's to say this place doesn't have any other surprises in store?'

'I agree,' Dale concurred. 'It's trying to flank us into trying to go out that way. For now, at least, we'd be better off staying put. It's only a few hours to go until dawn and Joey's end of shift. I have no doubt this place will fuck with us some more for its twisted entertainment, but at least we're not so confined here as we were upstairs. This place is playing a game with us; we just need to make sure that we stay alert and one step ahead.'

'A game's not so easy to play when there's no rules,' Grady grimaced as he raised the half-drunk water bottle for

Callum to have what was left. 'Trust me from experience, when you're fucking with those weaker than you, you do it because you know they won't fight back enough to trouble you. It's the watching of them finding new ways to struggle in vain that makes it more fun.'

Grady's statement was punctuated by another groan of pain.

'You need some alcohol to help stop any infection on that open wound,' Callum spoke.

Grady digested these words and nodded in agreement. He endured another wave of pain as he shifted his body and grabbed the half-drunk bottle of Southern Comfort that was within reach of him. He then began to guzzle the remainder of the contents.

'I meant to pour on the wound,' Callum spoke, frustrated. Even when he wasn't trying to, Grady fucking Daley was still finding ways to infuriate him.

'Maybe his way's better,' Dale mused. 'Best-case scenario, the booze knocks him out cold, especially with the speed he's downed it. Worst case, it at least takes some of the edge off his pain for a while.'

'It's fine,' Grady spoke after an almighty belch. 'There's still some more booze left by here.'

Grady made a reach for the can of Hoffmeister lager the other side of him and poured it over his wound. The yell of pain he emitted filled the hall of Davenport Manor.

'What on earth are you doing?' Callum berated.

'You said to pour alcohol on it,' Grady winced.

'Yeah, as in a spirit, not a weak as shit beer.'

'Well...' Grady began his counter to this brewing argument but then realised, for want of a better phrase, he didn't have a leg to stand on. 'I realise that now,' he finished the sentence with far less zeal.

CHAPTER SEVENTEEN

The radio show on Herts and Soul had now moved from Disco Dave's Night Owl Hour to the Power Hour, a slot dedicated to rock and metal.

The sharp incongruity between musical genres had been bridged by the opening track of the show, Kiss's 'I Was Made for Loving You,' which was a blend of both that shouldn't have worked as well as it did.

The presenter had stated after the record had finished that the time was a little past 04:00.

There were still another three hours to go before Joseph would come to the manor's doorway and realise something was awry.

The boys even dared to entertain the hope that when trying to radio through without success, Joey would venture to check on them and speed up their escape from this ordeal.

Unbeknownst to them, however, Joey had been radioing through at regular intervals as promised. Only each time, he had been greeted with Grady's voice accompanied by background sounds of the boys' laughter. As far as he was aware, they were having a much more enjoyable night than the dull one he was persevering through.

Ben had been awake for approximately twenty minutes.

Whether he'd been brought back around through the ill-effects of Dale's punch wearing off and the pain from his wound taking over, or by the rousing introduction of 'Heaven and Hell' by Black Sabbath blasting over the airwaves, he couldn't say—not that he could say anything now.

He tried moving his tongue to say something, out of a blend of instinct, hope and willpower, to see if he could train the muscular organ to do what had seemed like the simplest of tasks prior to his injury. But with it barely hanging onto the rest of the muscle, it was too flaccid to comply with his wishes.

All that escaped from his mouth, aside from some more diluted blood amongst the drool which had been storing up, was a collection of struggled sounds that betrayed what he was attempting to speak.

His wound upon his jaw had at least been fixed, albeit in a makeshift and clumsy manner, à la MacGyver style.

In Grady's backpack, he'd had a roll of heavy-duty steel tape he'd stolen from the building site when he first started his Youth Training Scheme.

His initial plan was that if he didn't enjoy his apprenticeship, instead of resigning the good old-fashioned way via a respectful letter, he was planning on sneaking up behind his insufferable prick of a foreman and wrapping the tape around his head, eyebrows included.

Sure, his boss would have been able to take the steel tape off, but not without sacrificing his eyebrows in the process.

As it was, Grady never did quit. Nor did he ever remember to take that roll of tape from the bottom of his backpack.

A section of this tape was ripped off and used as impromptu stitches. Sure, removing it would probably open the wound again, and likely remove a top layer of skin with it, but that was something they'd have to worry about in the future—if they had any future at all.

Even through all his treatments and diagnostics, despite there being numerous times he had felt the lows, the anger and the frustrations, Ben had never experienced such pity for himself as he was feeling right now.

Though he was no stranger to pain, this was a different kind he was now having to endure.

The physical pain of his wounds he felt sure he'd be able to suffer, yet it was the emotional pain which was stinging him the most. The feeling of selfishness that he'd wished they'd just let him die in that room so he could be done with this night and not have to sit here and watch his friends suffer their inevitable demise.

It was different for them to watch him die; they had become used to it. They had been watching his slow ebb for a while now, like a final scene in a movie gradually fading to black to signal the dawning of the end credits. But for him to have to watch their final scene, how was that fair?

He couldn't even speak to them now—all he could do was watch.

The thoughts of trying to repeat his suicide attempt were never far from his mind; his tongue was barely hanging on after all. Yet, as tempted by this as he was, it would be an ultimately fruitless endeavour. Dale was watching him like a fucking hawk and would be on him at the slightest sign. He had already threatened as much.

'Try any crap like that again, you wazzock, then you won't have to worry about swallowing your tongue, because I'd have ripped it off myself and shoved it so far up your arse, you'd be able to taste all the shit you caused us in there.'

Though Ben was sure this last part was delivered tongue-in-cheek, a phrase which he deemed rather ironic given his current situation, he still could detect the seriousness of the threat that was offered.

Ben couldn't even look him in the eyes. He couldn't look any of them in the eyes.

Tommy Iommi's mid-track guitar solo playing on the radio was abruptly cut short by the sound of static.

The boys braced themselves. They had come to learn that this wasn't some simple technical error or sudden loss of signal. Something was coming—they just didn't know what.

Accompanying the radio static were the collected screams of tortured beings. Grady recognised them as the same ones which had been on the other end of the walkie-talkie when they were in Room 42. These pained and nauseating sounds continued unwaveringly for several minutes, overwhelming the boys' senses. Each note of acute anguish and imploration for mercy these voices effused only served to distress the boys further.

When the screams finally did subside, so did the static. The familiar bassline of 'We've Gotta Get Out of This Place' had taken over.

Callum, Grady and Ben's gaze instinctively turned to Dale.

They all listened with attentiveness to the duration of the song, waiting on edge for something nefarious to be thrown their way. Like a toddler turning the crank of an old Jack in the Box, they anticipated the shock to come at any moment. The fact they were expecting it only served to make it worse.

'I'm really starting to go off this fucking song,' Grady attempted to laugh off the evolving tension, yet the disquiet was evident in his voice.

The track began its outro without incident, yet the boys' nerves failed to recede with it. A familiar voice began to speak over the track. It was DJ Rebel Ian. Only this time, his over-exaggerated hammy radio voice lacked the same zeal and cheese. If anything, it was subdued. It was humbled.

'It's just past 01:00 on 5th January 1991, and that was the Animals with "We've Gotta Get Out of This Place". This track is dedicated to the loving memory of Hertfordshire's very own local hero, Cpl Dale Reeves.

Cpl Reeves was killed in action two weeks ago in a heroic act of selflessness, sacrificing himself to save a group of civilians in the war-torn region of Kuwait City during the ongoing Gulf conflict. His bravery will never be forgotten. Cpl Reeves is survived by his mother Prunella Reeves.'

The broadcast turned to radio static once more, only this time, accompanying it there was the presence of women and children's screams amongst a duel of gunfire, followed by the sound of a muffled explosion.

Dale experienced the same feeling of brief but intense pain he had endured in Room 42 coursing through him as the sound of the explosion came through the radio speaker.

The radio returned to the Power Hour broadcast and

Black Sabbath's 'Heaven and Hell.'

Though it would be deemed blasphemy in some circles to silence Ronnie James Dio mid-vocals, Callum picked up the radio and hurled it hard against the floor—he had heard enough from this infernal radio.

The minor damage done to the radio wasn't enough; Callum began to stomp on it repeatedly until it was nothing but a collection of fragments and wires. Grady looked on approvingly at this act of destruction—that was at least until he realised it was his cherished radio that had been destroyed.

'If we get out of here alive, I'll buy you a new one,' Callum stated unapologetically as he read the look on Grady's face.

His concern was more over Dale than a busted radio.

'It's just this place fucking with you,' Callum attempted to reassure his friend. 'Trying to get inside your head and mess you up. Trying to let Davenport into your mind.'

Dale nodded without any real conviction. It was clear he wasn't convinced of his friends' assurances.

'Anyway, dude,' Grady contributed. His voice was still showing traces of a drunken slur. 'Even if this shit is true, if we somehow make it out of here, Davenport has screwed up big time and done you a major solid. If you know you're going to die in the army in a few years, just don't be in the army in a few years. Simple as that. You can't be killed somewhere you're not, right? This Davenport arsehole has just put a ten pence piece in your slot and given you an extra life.'

'Yeah, he's right,' Callum spoke with optimism. 'When we get out of here, all you have to do is discharge yourself when you get to base. You can do that within a certain period of your training, right?'

Dale possessed the deep look of pensiveness about him before he eventually spoke. He was resolute in his words.

'If we get out of here, I won't be seeking any discharge.'

'Why not?' Callum questioned. 'Even if this house isn't

screwing with you, why would you want to take that gamble? It's about playing the odds, and do you want your life to be the stakes?'

Though the words Ben attempted to say were indistinguishable as he tried to make his voice known, the pleading look on his face indicated he agreed with Callum.

'If I don't go, then those civilians might die?'

'So fucking what?' Grady snapped. 'You don't know them, and you don't owe them shit.'

'Even so, they're people. Innocents. How can you even begin to go on living your life knowing that a choice you've made has meant the deaths of other humans, maybe children? That kind of shit will drive you crazy. Besides, you never cheat the grim reaper out of his quarry for long. To be in debt to death is the worst kind you can owe, and he will always collect with interest.'

CHAPTER EIGHTEEN

'Hey, Ben dude,' Grady spoke. The discomfort was back in his voice now the pain-killing effects of the alcohol were weakening in his system. As well as the agony of his broken bones, he now also had the unwanted addition of a fledgling hangover. 'Are you doing okay? You don't look so good. Well, aside from the obvious, of course.'

Ben could only offer a pitiful smile and a half-hearted nod of the head.

Though he couldn't attest to how he looked, he couldn't doubt Grady's cause for concern. He was at the stage where he had been grateful for the constant sting of the wound to his tongue, since it was the only thing reminding him he was alive right now. The rest of his body, along with his mind, was lethargic and weak.

He shuffled over to Grady and gave him a gentle hug.

'Hey, don't go getting soft on me, Termy,' Grady berated benignly. 'Maybe it's a good job you can't talk right now. God only knows what soppy crap would come out of your mouth.' A mischievous smile then entered his face. 'I guess I'll have to do all the talking for you going forward.'

He adopted a semi-passable impression of Ben.

'Hey Grady, you're so much cooler than I am. I want you to have all of my video collection. I'm too much of a wuss to watch anything scarier than the Care Bears anyway.'

The pitiful smile on Ben's face turned to one more sincere and broader now, as he raised his middle finger to Grady. This did nothing to restrain his friend's mocking, however. If anything, it only encouraged him.

'This is the finger I like to stick up my bum,' he continued in his mock Ben voice. Even Dale and Callum were breaking into smiles now. 'I have to finger blast my arsehole since no girl that isn't inflatable will let me within a hundred metres of them. Grady, did you know my mum has got the hots for you? She told me herself—she wants to ride you like an untamed stallion and make you her bitch.'

Ben's laughs were thwarted by his wound and the discomfort that came with it, then he began coughing heavily. Such was the gusto with which these coughs came, it would have been easy for him to clamp down on his tongue and inadvertently finish the job his earlier attempt had failed at.

'Steady on there, champ,' Grady spoke, shifting into a serious tone.

Once the coughing had stopped, Ben removed his hands from his mouth; the blood on them was thick, dark and had not come from his wound. There was no point in him trying to hide it from his friends now—they had all already seen it. Suddenly, Grady didn't feel like joking around anymore. None of them did.

CHAPTER NINETEEN

'What time do you think it is now?' Grady asked.

'I'd hazard a guess at about five o'clock,' Callum replied.

'Just two more hours to go until Joey comes for us.' There were traces of quiet optimism in his voice—it wasn't matched by the rueful look on Dale's face.

'Yeah, and you can add all the extra time for him to get to town, get the emergency services, who'll then need to figure out a way to navigate the woods with the appropriate tools to cut that wall of beds open—if they even believe him, that is. Then you can add however long it'll take for them to actually get us out. Don't get any false hopes up, fella. We're not out of the woods yet—no pun intended.'

'I never want to see these damn woods again,' said Grady.

Ben had been deep in his thoughts about what would happen to them should they make it out of here alive. As far as his parents were concerned, he had been on a sleepover at Dale's. He had told them the truth about it being the last night Callum, Dale and he would be spending together and how much it would mean to him; it was just the rest of his ruse which had been a barefaced lie.

He didn't think it possible to feel more lousy than he already was when he pictured his parents' faces could they see them now—it was a whole new level of low he felt that even a limbo dancer would think impossible.

He was broken from his deep and guilt-ridden thoughts by a heavy itching on his leg. He began to scratch at the spot, yet it failed to satisfy the irritation. If anything, the areas that had been bothering him had become more widespread. The itching had now begun in the other leg too. He rolled up one of his trouser legs and could see what looked to be cockroaches crawling up his flesh.

He brushed off the bugs in a panic as he stood to his feet and called out to the others.

Although his words couldn't be fully distinguished, the panic in his voice could. He could see, ripping their way out of the fabric of the mattress, more of the bugs now, and not just roaches. There was an assortment of genera. Earwigs, beetles, spiders.

It wasn't only his mattress acting as a nest for these insects; the others were infested too. Callum and Dale began shaking their legs to try and free themselves of these trouser invaders, causing them to resemble a couple of demented Irish dancers in the process. Grady, however, was unable to stand, and the bugs were claiming him as their new nest.

'Get them off, get them off!' he yelled in hysterics. He rolled up the bloody jean and could see a variety of insects crawling over his leg—some of them were even shuttling around on his exposed shin bone, with the smaller bugs burrowing into his open wound.

He instinctively tried batting them off with his hand, yet as he struck his protruding bone, the cry he let out wasn't only one of panic, but of unadulterated pain.

With his judgement clouded by anguish, fear and alcohol, his next action proved to be more rash. He picked up the empty bottle of Southern Comfort and smashed it on the hard marble floor, turning it into a jagged weapon. He slashed the sharded remains at his wound to stab at the burrowing bugs.

Despite the pain he had inflicted on himself, he raised his hand again, ready to bring down a second blow. Yet he felt the strong hand of Dale grabbing onto his wrist to stop him.

'Dude,' he stated assertively. Though this was just a solitary word, it still managed to say so much more. 'Dude, don't be such a ruddy idiot. If you catch an artery with that glass, you're going to bleed out. You're playing into the house's trap.'

Dale scooped him up and carried him off the mattress. He gestured for Callum to check him over for bugs and get the rest of them off his legs. Not a favourable or easy task given how hysterical Grady was over the thoughts of these bugs upon (and inside of) him. Nor was it an easy task to get the insects off him due to how matted and sticky his bloody limb had become. Some of the clotted crimson plasma was starting to act as a natural alternative to flypaper.

Once he had been swept for insects, Callum aided Dale in physically supporting Grady. He was unable to put any weight on either his right broken ankle or his left snapped leg.

'Guys,' he winced. 'You can't carry me all night. Put me down on the ground. I think we're well beyond any chance of saving my leg from infection. Save your strength instead.'

'Shut up, you soft sod,' Dale defied. 'I've got enough strength to carry your sorry arse. How about you, Cal?'

'Not even breaking a sweat,' he spoke wryly.

Ben attempted to say something despite the pain and injury. Though they couldn't fully decipher what he was trying to say, they knew his meaning.

It was like Lassie trying to tell his owner Timmy was trapped down the well, only Ben was telling them he was willing to take a shift in supporting Grady's weight too once they began to flag.

'No offence, Termy,' Grady grimaced, 'but I don't think you've got enough strength in you to even support a football team. You don't look too good, pal. You're looking so pale you're making Casper the Friendly Ghost look like an Oompa Loompa.'

Grady could tell he had hurt his friend's pride at rebuking his offer, yet he remained resolute in not wanting Ben's help. It wouldn't be of benefit to any of them right now.

Any festering sense of awkwardness between them which may have had a chance to brew was halted before it even had a chance to develop by a frightened yelp.

'Guys,' Callum spoke with urgency and fear. 'Stay alert. I think this place is up to more tricks.'

'What you looking at, mucka?' Dale asked as he surveyed

the room as much as he could whilst holding up Grady.

'Black mould.'

The others followed Callum's finger as he pointed to a section of the black mould on the right-hand side wall.

They began to see it now as well.

The part of them that wished it was a trick of the eyes was overrun by the knowledge that the house was not done toying with them yet. The black mould looked to be moving on the walls, somehow shifting, congregating, forming a new shape—that of a figure.

'What was it your grandad said again?' Callum spoke, already knowing the answer. He just wanted validation that he wasn't going mad.

'That they're traces of the tortured souls of the departed trying to make their presence known to the living.'

'Did anyone think to tell them a nice little postcard is enough?' Grady attempted to joke, but the fear was dominant in his tone.

Ben made a noise that sounded like 'look' as he pointed to the other side of the hall. The mould he was pointing at was doing the same, as was all the other patches throughout the large room.

The twisted, mouldy figures began to peel themselves from the wall. The now-familiar screams of anguish and torment filled the room, only now they appeared to be coming from the unnatural shapes instead of the radio.

A loud thud could be heard, followed by an instant yell of severe pain.

'What the fuck!' Grady cursed at Dale. The shuddering at seeing these abominable figures had caused him to drop Grady through shock.

'Oh shit,' Dale professed upon realising what he had done, yet his eyes failed to break from the human-like forms of black mould.

As the figures began to assemble in the centre of the room, the boys couldn't help but notice the oddness of their forms. There was no depth to these one-dimensional forms;

it was almost as if they were shadows—bar the mouldy texture.

A group of these figures began to make their way forward slowly towards the boys. They could sense that even without eyes, the shadowy creatures were staring at them with insidious intent. They moved another taunting step closer. They were playing with their prey.

Though there were no mouths to these figures, the sounds of torment and agony escaped them somehow.

Another step closer they moved towards the boys.

'How do we fight shadows?' asked a panicked Grady.

'We can't,' said Dale ruefully.

Another step closer they came.

They were within a couple of metres of the boys now.

Throughout his friends' panic, Ben had been listening attentively to their screams. Just like that godawful screeching noise that accompanied the computer games when they loaded from the cassettes, the noises these beings—if he could even call them those—were shrieking in fragments of code. It was not a language of the living, nor the dead, but the in-between. Was it because Ben was so close to death himself that he could hear things in their tortured screams that his friends couldn't?

Though Ben couldn't be entirely sure, he thought he understood them enough to decipher their meaning. At least he hoped he understood them. Otherwise, the actions he was about to perform would be for nothing. His friends' chances would be for nothing.

Before the others could get a sense of what Ben was up to, he had already made his way in front of them and made a charge for the dark figures.

He'd let out a scream of pain as he ran through the figure directly in front of him and made his halt in the centre of the grand hall. The mouldy figures began to move away from the trio, and at greater speed.

Instead, they swarmed towards Ben, surrounding him before they attacked.

His friends could only watch on, helpless.

Approximately a dozen seconds later, the dark, mouldy shadows began to make their way back towards the walls.

'Ben!' Callum sobbed, distraught as he sprinted over to his lifeless body on the ground. He checked his friend for signs of life. There were none.

The sobs became wails now as he clung tightly onto the corpse.

If this were some fairy tale, the tears which fell from his cheeks and onto the friend he had loved so dearly would have been enough to bring him back to life. Alas, this was far from a fairy tale.

Callum lifted up the body as if he were an abominable creature carrying the heroine in peril in an old black-and-white B-movie and carried the corpse over to Dale and Grady—they too were crying over the loss of their friend, crying over all loss of any hope of getting out of here. Any last barriers of resistance their fortitude still clung onto had been broken down like a dam bursting its wall.

Though none of the trio dared say the words aloud, they each thought near-identical thoughts. Soon, this place would see them in the same state as their fallen friend.

It would seem to them that moment would be coming sooner rather than later as the grand hall was filled by the sound of a loud bang which caused each of them to jolt through surprise.

The sudden sense of shock rapidly turned to a lingering dread as the bang was immediately followed by a defiant but futile flicker of lights.

Then came absolute darkness.

'The generator's blown,' Dale stated.

'No shit, Sherlock,' Grady's impatient response came. 'Fuck this place.'

'Our torches,' Callum declared. 'They're back on the mattresses. I'll try and feel my way back there and find them.'

'No!' Dale defied with assertion. 'That's what this house

wants us to do. Divide and conquer. We stay together. No matter what it tries to throw at us.'

'Well, I ain't going anywhere,' Grady muttered. A sharp intake of breath betrayed his attempt at humour as a quake of pain shot through his injured leg.

Several minutes passed in the darkness of the room.

'I don't like that nothing's happening,' said Callum.

'Exactly,' Dale replied, his voice tight with tension. 'That's what this place wants. It's waiting until we're at our most confused, our most frightened, our absolute weakest. It wants us to let Davenport into our psyche.'

A sudden chill slithered through the room, raising gooseflesh on their arms. The breeze didn't feel natural—it moved with purpose, like icy fingers cruelly caressing their skin.

'Well, it's fucking working,' Grady admitted, his usual snark replaced by raw fear.

The malevolent wind curled around Callum, and with it came a voice he'd never heard before. A well-spoken yet slithering whisper. It was Davenport, and Callum knew it. Through the grief, the fear, the desolation, he had let him in.

Once his voice had been heard, Davenport's words clung to the walls of the boy's conscience, overwhelming his thoughts and manipulating them so that his voice and Callum's inner monologue had become indistinguishable.

Like the warriors hiding inside the Trojan Horse, now Davenport's voice was inside the enemy's domain, the assault was commencing with little resistance.

'Kill them both,' Davenport calmly commanded. 'The cripple will be easy. He deserves it to be slow and anguished for all he has done to you. Kill them both, and I will permit you to live to tell your tale.'

'Shut up,' Callum yelled.

Though the other two couldn't see it through the total darkness, he had placed his hands to his temples to help rid himself of the intruding voice.

Whenever he had seen people do this in those ridiculous horror films Ben used to love, he would scoff to himself over their stupidity at thinking this would make any difference to getting those iniquitous voices out of their heads, yet here he was doing the same futile thing.

'Who are you talking to, dude?' Grady winced with concern from his position on the ground.

Though these words had been spoken with genuine worry, by the time they had been absorbed by Callum, they had been as manipulated by Davenport as his besieged mind.

'Who are you talking to, IQ?' Grady's altered words swirled in his head with anger and bitterness. 'You need to man up right now instead of being a fruity fucking queer.'

The part of Callum which knew he was being tricked was overawed by the repressed anger inside him. The voice was right; Grady fucking Daley would be easy. He could stamp on his skull repeatedly and break it with as much ease as he had stamped on that wretched radio of his. Maybe he could dig his thumbs into his eyes and take his sweet time in gouging those fuckers out, relishing every squeal his longtime tormentor emitted, playing like a symphony of sadistic satisfaction.

The more he considered these violent acts, the more his fears turned to comfort.

'Cal!' he heard Dale's voice call out to him. 'What's going on, mucka? Speak to me.'

There was no need for Davenport to manipulate these words. With Davenport's darkness spreading through his thoughts, the unwarranted contempt was already simmering to the boil inside Callum.

Dale. Righteous Dale. Holier-than-thou Dale. Naïve to the true malice of the world Dale. About to have his fucking head caved in Dale. He had done nothing to deserve this brewing anger and resentment, but if Callum wanted to get out of this place alive, which he so desperately did, then his friend would merely have to be collateral damage.

If what the radio had told him about his fate was true, then he was already a dead man walking anyway; all he would be doing was speeding up the inevitable.

Though Callum was aware he was no match for him physically, the darkness was a good leveller, and he had Davenport to guide him.

What Callum didn't realise, however, was that he wasn't the only one Davenport was talking to.

'Hey, son,' a familiar voice came through to Dale. It was his father's.

With the voice being one he had so desperately yearned to hear again, Dale let it in with little resistance.

Once inside his mind, Davenport was quick to spread his corruption and sinister directives under the false guise.

'I don't have much time to speak to you, kid—before the other spirits know I'm here.

I need you to do one thing for me. I need you to kill your friends. It's the only way you can make it out of here alive.

No one in this world will miss a puff and a cripple, but it will miss you. You're destined to die a hero, not a loser in this place. Kill them both.'

'I can't,' he whimpered. 'They're my friends.'

'They're your burden,' his father's voice replied, though now it was a slither.

'What's going on?' Grady shouted to his friends, already suspecting they had let Davenport into their heads. It was as though the two of them were responding to conversations independent of each other.

Ben's recounting of the events of Hope and Glory came to mind, of how Davenport had been in the patients' ears, priming them for violence. Grady even felt a slight sense of offence at not being deemed a threat enough to have heard these voices for himself. Sure, his legs were incapacitated, but his fists were working fine, and as long as he had those, he could still fight if he had to.

The sound of a body hitting the floor shattered the silence.

In the pitch darkness, Grady could only listen as flesh met flesh—the wet smack of knuckles finding their target. He recognised the rhythm: Dale had Callum pinned, landing blow after blow.

Then a sickening sound came; it was the sound of the back of a cranium being bashed against the hard floor.

'Stop!' Grady bellowed. 'You'll fucking kill him!'

'I know,' Dale's voice came back, eerily calm. 'You're next, fella.'

Grady felt a boot come crashing down into his gut, taking all the wind from out of him. He instinctively placed his hands over his stomach, anticipating the next blow to be an action replay.

Maybe he would be able to grab the foot and take Dale off balance—it would be much more of an even fight if they were both felled.

Dale's boot came down again, though this time it was not on his stomach as he had expected. It had come down on his broken leg.

Grady's scream of pain filled the great hall. He anticipated the next brutal blow to come. Yet the sound of radio static accompanying a faint but familiar voice could be heard coming from the darkness.

'You've got to stay strong.'

'Ben?' Dale hesitated as he was about to unleash a punt to Grady's prone body.

'It's your fear and grief that is feeding him,' the voice continued. 'Mourn for me later, but please be strong for me now.'

'Ben! Where are you?' Grady spluttered. He could hear the voice too.

'I'm here. I'm with you. The spirits of the other poor souls he has wronged in this place are trying to run interference against him for me to speak to you. For me to save you. It's the only way. But I don't have much time. His spirit is much stronger than mine. But you three are strong enough together, even now.'

Dale could hear a groaning noise coming from the ground; it was Callum, he was still conscious, but barely. Guided by his groans, Dale joined him on the floor and lifted him up in an embrace. He made a feel for the back of his head to check for blood; thankfully there was none, though he wouldn't be surprised if he was suffering from a severe concussion.

'I'm so sorry,' Dale professed, fighting back tears. 'I don't know what came over me. I'd never hurt you on purpose, mucka, you know that. You've got to believe me.'

'I heard Ben,' Callum spoke groggily.

'So did I,' said Dale. 'He says we have to stay strong.'

'Easier said than done when you've just had the shit kicked out of you by your best friend,' Callum groaned.

The serpentine voice of Davenport started to ring in Callum's ears again.

'He lies. He has already tried to kill you once; he will try again, unless you kill him first.'

These words were countered by a softer, warmer voice. It was Ben again.

'Cal. Remember that time we hid pages from a dirty magazine inside loads of books in the local library? I'm not sure what was funnier, the outrage we caused, or the fact we had a lifetime ban from a library.'

Callum couldn't help but let out a giggle at this memory. Davenport's words were becoming more muffled now, losing itself in the static.

'Grady,' Ben's voice continued. 'Remember our first night together in the graveyard and the looks on the faces of the choir.'

'You mad termy bastard,' Grady laughed despite his pain. He then addressed the other two. 'Did Ben ever tell you that story?'

'He sure did, fella,' Dale replied. Though the others couldn't see it, he had a smile on his face. 'I hadn't heard him laugh that much for a long time when he told us.'

The malevolent voice of Davenport inside Dale and

Callum's mind was getting quieter now, more strained.

'Hey Dale,' said Callum. 'Remember the time we visited Ben in hospital that one time and we changed his medical board at the end of his bed to say that the nurse was to take his temperature rectally going forward? Ben was yelling blue murder when she actually tried.'

The boys' laughs were becoming harder now, as the trio began to reminisce over their fallen friend. The more time went on, it even got to the point where not all of the anecdotes were about Ben.

They hadn't even noticed that they couldn't hear his voice anymore - they couldn't hear any of the voices anymore, other than their own.

The sound of metal twisting could be heard in the background, yet they couldn't afford to pay it any heed. They couldn't relent with their reminiscing of happier times. They couldn't let the evil regroup or recharge.

The house was weakening, and they knew it.

CHAPTER TWENTY

The first shafts of light began to seep through the stained-glass window.

The barricade of beds remained in place in front of the entrance, yet they were untwined now. Some of them had already been flipped onto their buckled legs. Even though it would still take some work to clear a pathway, it would be manageable for Dale.

Though their relief at finally being given a way out was palpable, it still remained secondary to their thoughts of Ben as the daylight exposed his corpse.

'Remember what he said,' Dale ordered. 'Mourn later. We don't want to give strength to this house again with our grief.'

'Do you think he did that?' Grady spoke, pointing to the untangled barricade.

'I'm sure he did. Though I don't think he did it alone,' Callum concurred, somewhat groggily. His bell had been rung, that was for sure, but he was pretty certain there would be no lasting damage to his prized brain. 'I think he was aided by all the other fallen souls taken before their time in this place. I think that was why he let them take him. He knew they would be stronger that way. We'd all be stronger.'

'I think he knew he was always going to die in this place,' mused Grady. 'What was it he said again? When you knock on death's door for long enough, eventually it's going to let you in.'

******

The time was coming up to 07:00. Joseph still had an hour remaining of his shift. Something he had never been so pleased about in what he loathed to consider his career.

He was preparing himself to go into the manor, to see what mess the boys had left it in, and to ensure they left it spotless, or at least in the same state it was in when they had entered.

He radioed through to inform them he was coming in, yet there was no answer. This wasn't like the previous times he had radioed through, however. This time it appeared as though the other walkie wasn't turned on.

Joey let out an over-exaggerated sigh. If turning off the walkie was the height of their disobedience, so be it, he'd got off lightly.

He exited the hut and opened the gate on the security fence. That was the moment when he saw them.

'Holy fuck!' he proclaimed to no one other than himself.

The stocky fella, whose name he had forgotten, was carrying his brother in his arms. Even from a distance, he could see one of his feet was twisted the wrong way.

'Grady, what the actual fuck?' he shouted. He wasn't sure whether he was angrier or more concerned over his little brother's wound.

That reaction paled in comparison when he saw the ganglier lad, whose name he also couldn't remember, carrying the corpse of Ben.

The gangly boy didn't exactly look to be the picture of health either.

Joey rushed over to the group in panic. He didn't know what to say, how to act. There were so many questions running around in his head, and he wasn't even sure he wanted to hear the answers to them.

'It's true Joey,' Grady cried out. 'Everything they say about this place, it's fucking true.'

CHAPTER TWENTY-ONE

Upon the finishing of the telling of events to an exasperated Joey, they all agreed upon one thing. That what happened inside there would go no further. If more superstition and tales were spread about this place, it would only add more power to Lord Davenport and his unholy home by drawing more innocent but curious souls towards it.

It was agreed that Joey would report finding Ben's body outside the perimeter wall at the end of his shift. The severed tongue and gash upon his chin (minus the steel tape) must have happened when he fell awkwardly from trying to climb the perimeter fence in between Joey's patrols. Joey would offer his resignation with immediate effect over his failure to find Ben's body sooner.

As for Grady, as far as anyone not in the know was concerned, he had got drunk and was dicking about in the forest and fell from climbing a tree. It was a dumb enough and believable enough Grady fucking Daley thing to do.

Callum's bruises on his face courtesy of Dale would have been as a result of a heated argument between the two over some stupid topic which had been fuelled by more drinks than they could handle.

Neither of them, if questioned, was aware Ben had been planning to break into Davenport's, and as far as they knew, he had been spending the night down Grady Daley's.

Joey would enter Davenport Manor and retrieve the boys' backpacks and any other evidence of them being there as quickly as possible before the next shift would begin. He would blame the bed frames being in the grand hall on himself as part of a practical joke he was playing on the next person on shift.

As it turned out, such an excuse was not needed.

Upon Joey entering the manor, there was no sign of any bedframes, mattresses, or even the broken remains of the radio or the bottle of Southern Comfort.

Aside from the boys' backpacks, neatly lined up as if waiting to be collected, there had been no trace of anyone ever being there last night.

Joey ran in to retrieve the backpacks and just as quickly hightailed it out of there. Such was his haste, he had forgotten to close the door behind him.

He was halfway up the dilapidated pathway when he'd realised this and instinctively turned around. For the briefest of moments, he would even swear that in the ajar doorway, he could see a figure of a teenage boy smiling at him.

EPILOGUE

The year was 1991.

It was the year the Terminator met his judgement day, and Bryan Adams told us everything he does, he does it for you. It was also the year France and England amazingly broke through on the Channel Tunnel, and Freddie Mercury's body tragically succumbed to the AIDS virus.

Jeffrey Dahmer was arrested for being a very bad man, and Nirvana smelled like teen spirit.

Yet, for two men from the small town of Hulmsford, it was the year they attended the funeral of their best friend, Cpl Dale Reeves—a war hero who had died saving a crowd of civilians from a suicide bomber during the Persian Gulf War.

It had been a while since Callum had been to Hulmsford. His visits to his hometown were becoming more and more infrequent. Since the death of his mother from a short illness, he had never had much cause or desire to return, unless for a special occasion.

One of these rare occasions had been a few years earlier for the wedding of his old adversary, Grady fucking Daley, where he had been given the honour of being best man, along with Dale.

Grady, true to being the thoughtful man he had surprisingly grown into, had even made sure to schedule the wedding around Dale's service leave so the three of them could share their day together—and though they would reminisce about the good and the bad that had happened in their lives, they daren't talk about their night at Davenport Manor.

Grady had done well for himself, despite having only one leg. Such was the severity of the wounds and infection, it was unable to be salvaged. One leg's loss is another town's gain, however.

The townsfolk likened his newfound outlook on life to that of an overly-enthusiastic dog getting the chop—it had calmed him down significantly.

With his disability ending his bricklaying apprenticeship with immediate effect, less physical work was a necessity, and he began to take on more and more responsibility in his father's newsagent's.

Having a savvy instinct over what video rentals would do well, he even negotiated with his father to have full run of the video section and what titles to order—for a larger cut of the profits, of course.

Upon his father's retirement, he found himself running the newsagent's full time with Joey. With his newfound responsibility, he would go on to find newfound power too.

To the surprise of almost everyone, he would go on to become a town councillor, quite the accomplishment at such a young age. It was here he would thrive even more with his work for the community. What he lacked in academic acumen, he would make up for in fight—he had never lost that side of him. Only now, he was fighting for the people instead of against them. He had even launched the town's hugely successful anti-bullying programme.

One year after his marriage to Raquel Lewis (he finally offered to take her to a proper restaurant), his first son was born. Ben Dale Callum fucking Daley.

There had been an elephant in the room the night of Ben's christening which weighed heavily upon the trio of friends, none more so than on Dale.

The UK's involvement in the Gulf War had been all over the news, and memories of the radio broadcast inside Davenport Manor were never far away from any of their thoughts.

Though it was never spoken aloud, the three of them knew this would be their last night together.

Dale was stationed to Kuwait a week after, and in an identical letter he had sent to both Callum and Grady, it simply said the words:

Thank you, to my True Friends. You are my bridge.

Two months after, he was killed in the exact way he was told he would.

Dale had never married, never had kids, and had never even had a girlfriend.

Upon hearing some of his former squadron speak at his wake, despite being as dependable as they came for his squadron when it came to his service, once he was outside of uniform, it was said he was a distant and solitary man.

Callum had often wondered to himself if he'd already chosen to stop living the life he should have the night of Davenport Manor. Had he already let his fate devour him, and as a consequence, refused to let anyone else get close to him and get hurt?

Though his freshly cut marble gravestone said 1969–1991, Callum couldn't help but think that a large part of him died on 8th September 1984.

Callum was at the bar of the Hulmsford Social Club where the wake was being held. He had ordered himself a JD neat.

The barman had been none other than Bradley Hale. He was balding, overweight, and underpaid.

Callum wasn't sure whether the bitterness over serving him was because this incredible queer's life had turned out to be distinctly more successful than his, or whether Bradley hadn't known any success at all. 'Oh how my heart wails,' Callum thought with sarcasm.

He thanked Bradley aloud for the drink, and then silently for the sense of superiority, before hearing the unmistakeable tapping sound of Grady approaching—it wasn't hard with the hard wooden floor of the function room.

'Where's my drink, fuckface?' Grady spoke with a wry smile.

'I didn't want to buy you one in case you got legless,' the reply came, to which Grady gave a hefty laugh and a high five.

'Been saving that one up for a while, have you, pal?'

'Yeah. Unfortunately, that's the extent of my amputee repertoire.'

'I expect a new one for the next time you feel morally obliged to come down. I'm going to have to work on getting Raquel up the duff again, just so you have an excuse to come back.' Grady turned his attention to Bradley. 'Four doubles of Archers neat, please. Two for us and two for our best friends who can't be with us tonight.'

The barman placed the four highballs of Archers on the bar.

'Peach Schnapps for m'lady,' Grady teased with affection as he handed one of the glasses to Callum.

Though he didn't give the command, they both knew the drill. They counted to three before downing the spirit.

'To Dale and Ben,' Callum toasted as he handed another glass to Grady. They repeated the ritual.

'Jesus Christ that stuff is vile. I don't know why you like it so much,' Grady rued.

'I've never liked it. I don't know why you keep thinking I do, you homophobe.'

Grady smiled briefly then looked a bit more serious. Callum hated this expression on him.

'Say, Cal, I've been wanting to ask you something, dude,' Grady spoke nervously. 'Is everything OK with you? You don't look well.'

'I'm fine. Just the stress and emotions of today, I guess.'

Grady didn't want to push further, but he knew Callum was lying to him. He looked pale, gaunter, and had spotted a couple of lesions on him when they had embraced each other upon their reunion earlier.

****

The hour was coming up to midnight and Callum had found himself walking through the Hulmsford forest alone.

Whether it was the abundance of alcohol still rife in his system, or the illusion of nostalgia, but he could picture Dale by his side and Ben and Grady in front of him back when they were still teens. Callum began darting his torchlight around as if it were a firefly, giggling mischievously as he did so.

'Hey,' a surly-sounding security guard called out to him. 'You're not supposed to be out here, this is private property.'

'You're no Joseph,' Callum slurred. 'He was the best goddamn security guard this place ever had.'

'I don't even know who the fuck that is. Now are you going to beat it, or am I going to have to call the cops?'

'There's no need for that, my good man. How about I call on a few of my good friends instead? They're all called Christopher Wren.'

The security guard looked more confused now.

'Let me guess. You don't even know who that is,' Callum sighed as he pulled out his wallet and produced ten fifty-pound notes.

'What's this?'

'My security clearance,' Callum spoke.

******

The generator had been in the same spot as when he had last been in here. He hadn't even tried pulling the choke cord to power up the generator when the lights to the foyer came on. The manor was pleased to welcome back an old acquaintance, it would seem.

Callum reached into his jacket pocket and pulled out Ben's old Polaroid camera. He didn't know why he had asked Ben's parents if he could have it when he had gone to visit them a couple of days after his death and had seen it on the coffee table in their living room.

'He wanted people to see the world how he saw it,' his mother had said as her trembling hand passed it over to Callum. 'Despite the shit hand he'd been dealt with,

Benjamin still saw the world as a wonderful place. And he saw you as a wonderful friend. I can't think of anyone better to have it.'

Callum raised the camera lens at himself and pressed the button for the photo to be taken. He retrieved the photograph and placed it in his pocket while he waited for it to become fully developed. He sat down in the centre of the grand hall, the same spot they had chosen seven years ago. After five minutes had passed, he retrieved the photograph from his pocket.

A warm smile entered his face as he examined the Polaroid. Standing beside him in the photograph, with a beaming smile and his arms wrapped fondly around him was Ben. A second and not so welcoming figure was also present in the background. Davenport.

Callum emitted a deep, weary sigh and stood to his feet. This was going to be a long night.

This was going to be his last night.

THE END

ABOUT THE AUTHOR

Steve McElhenny is short, Welsh, and hairy.

ALSO AVAILABLE BY THE AUTHOR

Lethal Dangerousness
Lethal Forcefulness
Draculand
Avenging Aranis: Episode One – The Flames of the Inferno
The Girl with a Porcelain Face
Fire McGuire
Kingshire Falls
Mockingbird
The Headphones
The Joke
Fear Goggles
Human Statues
The Man who thought he was a Cat

Printed in Dunstable, United Kingdom